This book should be returned, or renewed, on or
before the latest date shown on this label.

**Wandsworth Libraries
24 hour Renewal Hotline**
~~01494 777675~~

Wandsworth
1900 - 2000

L.749A (6.2000)

SILVERTAIL BOOKS • *London*

This edition published by Silvertail Books in 2017
www.silvertailbooks.com
Copyright © Anne Patterson 2017

1

The right of Anne Patterson to be identified as the author of
this work has been asserted in accordance with the
Copyright, Design and Patents Act 1988. A catalogue record
of this book is available from the British Library. All rights
reserved. No part of this publication may be reproduced,
transmitted, or stored in a retrieval system, in any form or by
any means, without permission in writing from Silvertail
Books or the copyright holder.

978-1-909269-80-4

For Sam and Molly

1

'Yes,' I hear myself say, though I mean 'no.' I don't want tea. I have fallen asleep in a café.

'Sugar?'

'Yes.'

I'm saying 'yes' again as if I have no choice. Sweet tea, that's worse. And I'm even misusing the one word my brain will let me say. I have such a headache. And the tablecloth is folded over me. God, what's happened? For some reason the tea is in a plastic cup with a hole in the top and a straw poked through. The waitress... hang on, she's not a waitress. She's a nurse. There are two of them – but my vision is a bit fuzzy. No, it's not just my vision. One comes on either side of me, so I can't be seeing double. They lift me up and fold me forward. There is a clank and click of metal behind me and the soft plump of pillows being arranged. I'm sitting up now and suddenly I'm in hospital. It's not even the local hospital. I spent enough time visiting my mother there to know its layout. Where am I? Where am I? Does anyone know I'm here?

I can't speak. When I try, I sound like I'm learning a new language. The nurse thinks I am asking about the scarf on the bedside locker.

'Your husband left it.' The nurse talks to me slowly and loudly as if I am a foreigner. Then she drops the volume and speaks to her colleague across me. 'The husband was leaving as I came on this morning. Sweet. He must have sat with her all night. Not bad-looking either. A bit younger than her, or it could be the stroke. It doesn't improve your looks.'

Now I'm really confused. My husband died years ago. I think

I've been drugged. Christ, I can't have remarried and forgotten about it, can I? Perhaps they think I'm someone else.

'Just sip. It might be a wee bit hot, though I put extra milk in it.'

The nurse holds the straw near my mouth and I struggle with it like a dog being teased with a biscuit. Milky, sweet tea, like my daughter Jackie drinks. My idea of hell but I'm gasping so I'll drink it. The nurses have gone now and I'm sliding down the bed and over to one side. I see a name-band at my wrist. The label has slipped round towards my pulse. The hand is weighted down and I can't seem to... I can't move my arm at all! The other one has a drip attached. How did I not notice that? I move that arm. The wrist-band shifts round and I see with relief that it's my name. *Maureen McCormack*. I haven't been kidnapped and given a new identity by the man with the green scarf. I'm not able to lift my hand though. That is something to panic about. I can't even move myself up the bed. Am I drunk or drugged? God, I feel so tired.

I see sparks of light from the corner of my eye. I want to tell the nurse to get a fireguard but I can't. I think the lights are in my eyes so I close them.

And now I'm in a field. It's not really a dream but a memory. The field was small and the hedges were high – an old-fashioned sort of field, not tidied into efficiency like the fields of today. It was late summer. I was collecting rosehips for my mother. She had given me an old enamel kettle to collect them in. The rose-hips made a satisfying metallic noise when I dropped the first few in but as it filled up, the noise deadened and disappeared. Mother had gathered several bowls full but my kettle was still only filled up to the spout. The briar thorns scratched the backs of my hands several times. I showed the scratches to my mother. She unfolded the cuff of my cardigan and pulled the sleeve over my hand to give some sort of protection. I wanted to be fast like my mother and collect bags and bags of rosehips for the jelly. I was three years old and didn't yet have the speech to explain my feelings of frustration. Again Mother reminded me not to eat them.

'They look lovely but they're full of wee burrs that'll stick in you and kill you. Don't put them near your mouth.'

I knew the story of the snake in the Garden of Eden and the apple, so I was wary of fruit – but surely a lick couldn't harm me. I wouldn't bite into it. When she was emptying her bowl into the big cloth bag, I stuck my pointy tongue out and licked, expecting the red pod to taste like sweet rosehip jelly...

*

I must have fallen asleep and dribbled. It's the sort of thing you do in church and hope no one has noticed. The light is changing and there is a tinny whoosh. The screens are being drawn. An older woman with a bigger and sillier hat, perhaps she's the sister, comes in with a medical student. No, he's not; she introduces him as the consultant.

"Can we bring some medical students in to have a look at you, Mrs McCormack?" he asks in another booming talking-to-foreigners voice.

"Yes," I say in my tentative new 'four-gin-and-tonics-too-many' voice because I can do nothing else. They are appearing through the gap as if for a curtain call. One, two, three, four, five. It's got to stop. There are six of them. I am so tired.

'Mrs McCormack was admitted semi-conscious. No medication with her. Found slumped in the car. Luckily she was parking.' (Special voice for me.) 'You're a very lucky lady. Can anyone tell me what we have here?'

The gang in the white coats are silent

'More details. Left-sided paralysis. Almost total aphasia.'

3

'CVA,' someone mutters, as if they don't want to be teacher's pet.

'Look at the face.' They are leaning towards me and seem to be changing form like a line of reflections in a hall of mirrors. I begin to cry and I can't stop. The sister sits by the bed and puts her hand on my arm above where the drip goes in. In the background the consultant murmurs, 'Emotionally labile,' as if it's an insult. The sobs are tugging at my body. It feels as though I am being lifted and then dropped again and again. I don't even feel organised enough to work out all the things I should feel unhappy about.

'You're tired and a bit shaky,' says the sister in 'the voice'. 'It's perfectly natural. It's the shock. You've had a bit of a stroke, dear.'

A bit of a stroke? How bad? People talk about a slight stroke or a massive stroke. Which is this? She answers my silent question.

'We don't know how bad it is. Things take a while to settle.' She reaches starchily across me for a tissue and dabs at my face as if trying to remove a stain. 'We'll need to re-site that drip and then the physio will be around to assess you. I'll get a couple of nurses to pop you on your side and make you more comfy.'

Two nurses come and fold me forward. They click the back-rest away and position me on my side. Pillows are arranged under my knee and arm and along my back. I suddenly feel much happier and more comfortable and smile my thanks. The nurse looks concerned.

'Sorry, have I hurt you? Are you okay?' The smile obviously doesn't look like a smile.

'Yes,' I say and feel like laughing but instead drift towards sleep again.

*

Before I open my eyes I smell my sister, Shirley. All the perfume and hair-spray can't hide the smell of that mossy little girl who leaned against me in garden hideouts. Grassy knees up near our chins, while our mother pretended to have lost us. I feel very tearful, thinking of how we stopped being close once we hit adulthood. As if we had to choose between being sisters and being wives. Now perhaps I've missed my chance.

Shirley is looking at me intently.

'What were you doing in Belfast?' she asks. 'You never mentioned it. If Doctor Kelso hadn't phoned we'd have had no idea. I had to race over to your place for Jackie coming off the bus.'

'Yes,' I say, but even if I could speak I couldn't tell her why I was there. I hate driving and only go to the city if absolutely necessary. I am worried about Jackie but my sister tells me she is all right. I was worried about the farm but they've organised all that too. My sister can certainly talk. I don't need to be able to answer questions. She tells me everything right down to what flavour of dog food Tara has been given. Oh God, I've realised I've suddenly forgotten my sister's name – but I can remember the dog's. I feel exhausted by the time she leaves.

Nurses come and go. They empty my catheter bag. I've been worried about that. My right arm is cuffed and squeezed to get my blood pressure. I am approached with a thermometer.

'We'll pop this under your tongue and then we'll sit you beside the bed for a nice wee cup of tea.'

It's hard to let yourself be lifted. I want to help. Not since childhood has my body been completely supported by other people. That sort of helplessness and letting go has to be re-learned. It's a bit like swimming: if you struggle above the water, it will make you more likely to sink. I have to think about floating. They are holding me like the water.

*

5

I am awoken again. I don't remember drinking tea. There are two people by my bed. They smile and tell me they are going to ask me some questions but I am not to worry. I don't know if they are doctors. For a moment I wonder if they are Jehovah's Witnesses because they have that clean-living look.

'Who is the current Prime Minister?'

'Yes' I say, knowledgeably. 'Yes.'

They do not know that I am trying to say Tony Blair. I wonder do they check patient's political beliefs or will committed republicans always score low in this test?

They are conferring at the end of my bed and scribbling on some paper.

'I want you to tell me what year it is, Mrs McCormack,' the male doctor says slowly. He points to dates in circles on his page and goes through them. 'Is it 1996? 1988? 1997? 1998, 1995?'

I say yes after 1998. I am confident that I am right but also he smiles and raises his eyebrows as he names 1998. They seem happy.

Now they are showing me pictures of mice.

'Which mouse is under the table?"

I point to the mouse in the left-hand picture. Now they want to know which mouse is behind the table. I point at a different mouse. They are smiling. I am so tired.

*

Getting fed is awful. The mince and potatoes take on a life of their own. The nurse is bored and talking to the woman behind her. She puts practically the whole spoon in my mouth and pulls it upwards until the handle touches my nose and the bowl of the spoon jars against my bottom teeth. By the time she starts the pudding she is really in a hurry and I scarcely have time to swallow between bites. Swallowing seems to have changed from a natural reflex to something as complicated as changing a plug. She has put some blue paper towelling across my chest as a bib. As she moves the tray, I look down with disgust at the slavered shepherds pie and ice-cream. A fresh piece of paper towelling is dampened and the nurse wipes my face rather roughly and walks off. I feel guilty about all the times I did the same to Jackie when she was little.

Another uniformed figure arrives. She stands in front of my chair, feet unnaturally far apart for a woman, her hands resting on her solid hips.

'Ah Mrs McCormack, you're a right-sider, aren't you?'

This confuses me for a moment, because in this part of the world Protestants describe themselves as 'digging with the right foot' and call Catholics 'left footers'. Then I realise that she is referring to the side of my body I can't move.

'I should have been here earlier. I can't really haul you around when you've just eaten, can I? I'm your physiotherapist. We'll just have a chat for now.' She glances at her sheet of paper. 'You've got a bit of a problem with the old speech at the moment, so I'll do the talking.' She smiles. 'That's the way I like it.' She has a matter-of-fact Princess Anne way of talking, but I like her. 'Now you might know some of this, but I've no way of telling and no one in this place explains a thing to patients. Your stroke has affected the left side of your brain which controls the right side of your body. It also controls the language centre and that's why your speech has gone for the moment. But they caught you early and whacked you full of Warfarin, which thins the blood; you probably know it as rat poison. If your stroke is caused by a blood clot in the brain, it will shift it. Enough information. I'm off to get somebody to give me a hand.'

I am glad she told me where she was going. Before, I was left like a baby bird, beak straining out of the nest waiting for mother.

She returns with a nurse to help me into bed. I feel drunk. They put me on my normal side with a pillow under my floppy top arm. She stretches my fingers out one by one until they are splayed out as if she is planning to get a pencil and draw round my hand. She puts a pillow under my knee and one at my back. It really is like being wrapped in cotton wool. She sits down in front of me and says goodbye. I look at her upside down nurse's watch. It says either a quarter to or a quarter past five.

Gradually the length of the ward is unfurling before me. It's misty like a reflection in a dusty mirror. I am aware of voices near the door which is three beds away.

'I'm sorry sir, but visiting time is between seven and eight-thirty,' says an officious little nurse with two stripes on her hat. The man is hidden in the shadows at the edge of my vision but I know the voice.

'I'm here to see Mrs McCormack. I'm her GP.'

The nurse steps back. For a moment I think she is going to curtsey.

'I'm so sorry.' (To have thought you were a mere mortal and not a doctor, I think to myself.)

He comes towards the bed in his shaggy corduroy and tweed uniform.

'She's doing very well,' says the nurse. 'Shall I go and get Sister?'

'No, it's fine. Don't bother yourself.'

'Do you want to see the registrar? I could bleep her.' The nurse is standing at the end of the bed fiddling with a chart. Clearly she doesn't know how to cope with this scenario.

'Maureen's a friend too. I want to have a chat first.'

'She can't talk, you know,' the little nurse blunders on.

He shuts his eyes and moves one hand in an open-fingered wave which looks as if he's pushing her away.

People on either side of me are having things done so their

screens are round. I am sheltered on three sides. The faded green meadow of the hospital curtains casts a light which sucks the colour from his face. He sits on the bed and holds my normal hand, now free of its tubes and bandaging. He holds it in a tight grasp and the needle bruise hurts but I am glad of the sensation. I am probably imagining the tears in his eyes but mine are real enough. Drip, drip, dripping over my nose and cheekbone into the pillow. He has one hand and the other I can't move.

'Maureen, I was here when you came in. I happened to be going through the A and E entrance for a meeting and I saw you on the trolley. I thought you were dead. God, I shouldn't say that, but you've always looked so healthy even when you're ill.'

He puts his other hand on mine so I am sandwiched between them, as if we are two world leaders in a photo call after signing a peace treaty. Warm hands, soft for a man. Nails just the right length. Fine dark hairs curling round his watch strap. A cream cotton shirt cuff appearing under his herringbone tweed jacket.

'Maureen, I'll get you home.' I hear him breathe in. He turns away and lifts his top hand to touch his face. 'It's not too late.' There is a pause and he says it again, quietly and slowly. 'It's not too late.'

The sister appears. 'Oh dear, getting upset again, are we?' I hear her say, as if addressing a mischievous child. 'We find that, especially with our younger strokes,' she confides to the doctor and then she asks him in a loud whisper: "Have you been trapped?"

Dr Kelso looks baffled for a second, then says: 'No, no, I'm not busy – I can stay a while. Can you tell me how things are going?'

'Shall we go to my office? You could probably do with a coffee.'

'I'm sure Maureen would like to hear what's happening too.'

'Right, I'll get the notes,' says Sister with a sullen twist in her voice.

Disappointed not to get him in her room, I think. He is still attractive for someone in his early fifties. About my age, or a little older. He's probably starting to lose a little hair and there are flashes of grey above his ears but Sister obviously thinks he is worth fishing for.

2

They take me for a bath today. I couldn't have imagined how they'd do it. I am put on a strange chair which looks like a toilet seat on wheels. My nightie is scrunched up at my waist. They wind a blanket round my legs. The chair arms are slotted into place to enclose me. In the bathroom, there is the sound of clicking and levers behind me. My chair is attached to some sort of hoist. No one tells me what is going on. The nurse takes my night-dress off and then winds a handle with a ratchety noise. I am left suspended in mid-air over a foamy bath while the nurse talks through a slightly open door about the breakfast break rota.

I am face to face with myself in the mirror. I look old and pulled to one side. My dark and usually wavy hair is flat and turned under instead of fluffed out a bit. I try smiling. It doesn't look too grotesque. It is still a smile. One of those 'you-win-some-you-lose-some' sorts of smiles. I comfort myself. It wouldn't scare children.

I relax into the bath. Not quite hot enough – but I am not here to luxuriate. No lying back reaching for the hot tap with my big toe while I hold onto my library book. A quick in and out. Like a sheep dip. I feel a draught. Another nurse walks in.

'I'll give you a hand. The physio's here for her.'

She dries me so carefully; it is as if she is scared I will rust.

'She's doing well,' the first nurse says across me. I feel stronger.

The nurses giggle as they take me back to the bed. The chair wheels have wonky-trolley syndrome, and in the end I approach the bed backwards to find the pear-shaped physio flicking through someone else's copy of *Take a Break*.

'They tell me you're doing well. I'll have her on the bed, please. Today we're going to practise rolling.'

The nurses leave us alone behind the screens.

'We have to go back to basics. Sorry to sound like a Conservative Party slogan... I'm going to call you Maureen, if that's all right? So I can call you Mrs McCormack when I get strict.'

I laugh and it sounds like a real laugh. She looks at me differently. I thought of things people say about my Jackie. 'The light's on, but there's no one at home.' The physio can tell now that there is someone in, even if I can't answer the door.

Rolling. We're going to practise rolling. When she says 'we' she means just me, of course. It's the 'NHS we' as opposed to the 'royal we'. Rolling doesn't seem very complicated, does it? But today it has turned into a skill like flying. It's as if half my body is real. The other half is something else, someone else's body that you're watching in a mirror and trying to move by remote control. After a few goes I can roll onto the affected side, but getting back over on the other side is like roller-skating uphill. I have several goes at it.

She is very patient,

'Lead with your eyes, Maureen – that's it. Pretend you're trying to reach a nice piece of chocolate cake and a cup of tea. Use your good arm. That's it, extend it out. Get your arms over and your legs will start to follow. Think of the cake, Maureen. Lead with your eyes. That's it. LOOK AT YOUR LOCKER, Mrs McCormack. Nearly there. Nearly there.'

In the end she has to pull my bottom half over. I am tired and disappointed but she seems really pleased.

'That was a really good start. I think twenty minutes is enough for this morning.'

'Yes,' I say. Twenty minutes? She has been with me for at least three hours, surely? My time thing seems to have gone a bit. Before she leaves, she gets me into position again, like an artist arranging a reclining life model for a sitting.

*

I probably dozed off, and the clatter of trays being pulled out of a metal trolley wakes me.

The woman in the next bed announces loudly, 'I didn't order this.'

I overhear the nurses complain that she always does this. I think she's a bit confused.

I believe I'm still getting food ordered by the person who was in the bed before I arrived. A menu card has appeared on my locker and perhaps I can get my sister to help me with it. Macaroni cheese for me today. They expect me to eat it by myself. Unhampered by a drip, it should not be too difficult, but I somehow feel I am doing one of those games where you stand behind someone and pretend your arms are their arms. Yet I am managing to get the food to my mouth. I feel more balanced. I have more of an idea of where I am today. I mean that physically – but it could also be said about my mind. I'm having a delicious cup of sweet tea now. I had a gesturing attempt to dissuade the tea lady from putting the sugar in, but I think she thought I was urging her on.

The loo is one of those disabled ones with an abnormally high seat. I feel like a child as they shuffle me back towards it, sharp plastic cutting into the back of my legs. Legs. I did say legs? I am starting to feel as if my leg is part of me again – my 'bad leg', as they call it, as if it is wilfully disobedient. The disabled toilet is next to a room with buckets and a big machine. It has a faint smell of churches. Stale flowers in metal vases.

Back in the ward I get a whiff of something like nappy-rash cream overlying the disappearing school-dinner smell of the lunch trolley. Other smells, more unpleasant, I won't talk about. Why is smell so important now? I'm stuck here, so I suppose I've got to make the most of every sensation open to me in my environment.

Here's my sister. She's called Shirley. How I hated our names. Maureen and Shirley. It doesn't matter now, but when I was a teaching student surrounded by Lynns and Lydias I used to mumble it and hope no one would ask me to repeat it. Shirley has a huge bag with her. She seems to have borrowed night-dresses from half the country – but no, they are her own personal emergency hospital supply. Let's hope she's not admitted, or they'll come to strip me to get something for her to sleep in.

'I know you laugh at me over this sort of thing but it's better to be prepared. Here, I've brought you some nice soap and deodorant. Claire insisted I bring in a book of poems from her shelf. I said you probably couldn't read but here you go anyway. She's not the most practical, but she means well. They said you ate your own lunch so that's nice. I'm bringing Jackie tomorrow, if that's all right, and Claire is thinking of coming over home soon. Is it all right if Jackie comes? I don't want to upset her.'

I nod my head.

'I've tried to explain that you can't talk but she doesn't really listen. She wants to see you anyway.'

I give a sort of general questioning look to glean more information.

'And you're not to worry about anything on the farm. Jim is in charge. He's on top of everything.'

I smile. I doubt that Jim really did feel he was in charge. Laid-back, lovely Jim who helped on our farm and brightened my life, was probably suffering from having Shirley monitoring his every move. I point out the menu card and she holds it at arm's length.

'I've no glasses. Is it for ordering your meals? Here, I have a pen.'

She finds my glasses in the locker and between us we manage to fill it in. Shirley ticks the options I nod at. What is Glasgow pie, I wonder? I'll find out tomorrow.

'You look a hell of a lot better. I was worried about you. That's why I told Claire to come home, but it'll be nice to see her anyway.'

I'm glad I've got my sister. Who else have I got? I have Jackie, my Down's Syndrome daughter. Walter, my husband, is dead nearly seven years. I have Claire my niece. Three women to visit me and the mystery man who left his scarf, or did I dream that?

And Dr Kelso came yesterday – or was it the day before? The problem of my mind becoming clearer now is that I now realise how confused things were before. Do GPs usually come and see their patients in hospital? He told the nurse that he was my friend too. The thing is, I've been half in love with this man for years now. I remember when he first came to town. All the women were mad about him. But he had a beautiful wife, and then twin boys arrived to further protect him from unwanted attention. I wouldn't want people to think I was the sort of person who developed crushes on doctors like someone from an episode of *Dr Finlay's Casebook*. This wasn't like that. It wasn't one-sided. There were times when I thought, Maybe if I hadn't been married... if he hadn't been married... if he hadn't been my doctor. Well, it's too late now.

'Here, why are you crying? Don't worry about us. Oh God, what have I said? Are you okay?' Shirley is half-standing now and looking for a nurse.

'Yes,' I say and nod my head, glad that I don't have to explain myself.

Shirley watches me in silence. 'I've got a pen and paper. Could you write, do you think?' She's always found it difficult to deal with tears. She was hopeless when Jackie was born.

Can I write?

Shirley puts the pen in my left hand and brings out a cheap orange and red child's sketch-pad. She's probably bought it especially for me. It has a 35p price sticker on it. She's bought it from McMullan's. She folds the cover back and it gives a snap when the cardboard breaks away from the stack of coarse grey paper. What will I write? That I feel not bad. That I can hear and understand but just can't speak the words. That things are a little confused and that I can't remember what I was doing when I took ill. Or will I write *I love you Shirley, why did we not talk when we had the chance?*

I grip the pen in the unfamiliar hand and scribble to get it started but then I can't write. I can visualise writing, I can move my hands but I can't put the words on the page. It's like being asked to write in an alien script. This is very depressing. Shirley is at a loss now. She writes *CAN YOU READ*? I nod and say yes.

I feel completely sealed off from everyone. Even if I learn to walk I might never communicate again. The things I'll never say. The things I'll never know. Here is a list:

Why are the things on the end of walking sticks called ferules?
How do you pronounce Zeitgeist?
How do you bake perfect scones?
Is Shirley happy?
Does she know anything about the first baby?
Does Tom Kelso know I love him?

Shirley starts talking again. She tells me they have a supply teacher to take my class at the school.

'She drives the whole way from Lisburn; she's that desperate for work.' Then there is silence. Even prattling away about nothing gets difficult when there's no response. 'Oh, here's a wee card from your evening class. Mary McGovern came into the shop to leave it for you. I'll open it, will I? Look, home-made. That's a bit mean, though I suppose they thought you'd appreciate it as you teach them.'

She holds the card five inches from my face, forgetting that I too have started to hold things at arms length to focus. It's Mary's work, I can see – a pretty little water-colour of a bridge. It's a bridge near home. I cross it every day going to work. The scale is a bit wrong so it looks like a tiny bridge over a rushing torrent but she's got a good eye. Inside they've all signed it. Meta, Betty, Eileen, Sandra and finally Elizabeth Kelso. Elizabeth's writing isn't like the others, scratched on with a passed-around Biro. She has signed it with a swishy, inky fountain pen as if she were signing a royal decree. Round here, being married to the doctor means something – and she knows it.

I look at the bridge again and feel stuck on one side of it, able to watch and hear but not to cross to those on the other side.

'They're nearly all transferring to the patchwork class. Its numbers are low... or else they can have a refund. They're keeping their options open for the spring term. I didn't know what to tell them.'

Shirley looks worried. She's probably wondering what's going to happen to Jackie as well as to me. Who'll look after us – two damaged women? Does Shirley feel she has to pay me back for having Mother living with me for all those years?

I miss Jackie, sitting right close to me while watching television. She still has no idea of personal space. My woman toddler, bleeding every month but still holding my hand when we go to the big Marks & Spencer's at Sprucefield. I miss her delight at favourite puddings when we're out and her infuriation at my rationing of sweet stuff when we're at home. I love the way she comes out with phrases like 'I need a calorie controlled diet' and sings along to 'I feel like chicken tonight' or quietly picking up things she hears on the news 'UN... UN peace-keeping force'.

She loves things that children grow out of, like walking through a line of washing, feeling cool sheets brushing past her cheeks and slipping over her head. She begs to have the car window open to feel the wind pulling her hair back, gasping at the force of it until her ears get sore. I've had to tell her things that ordinary kids would have realised. You don't hug everyone. I managed to tone that down to vigorous hand-shaking. She likes to carry things in the hood of her jacket. She doesn't like her pockets cluttered. She looked ridiculous with her hands in her pocket and her coat pulled tight along her throat, weighted down by her purse and her packed lunch. Her cousin Claire bought her a stylish mini-rucksack which she reluctantly uses now.

Shirley is still talking. I haven't heard so much talk about very little outside the commentary on a royal wedding. She tells me about Claire. She's in Scandinavia, she says, as if it's a country. I picture Claire among tall, very blond people.

'She's in some advert. Very lucrative, but not what she wants. Nearly thirty and she still wants arty and no pay. Still, what can I say? I'm only her mother. I have a notion she has a new fella, but sure she tells me nothing.'

Shirley chats about the journey and the car and then the MOT she must organise and the Calor gas that's running out and the water rates, and I realise she is not having a conversation, she is making a list of all the things she needs to do. She is a woman under pressure.

Suddenly, I think she must sense I am concerned.

'It'll be grand,' she says hastily. 'I just need to get myself into a routine. Get Jackie to put her clothes out in the evening. Maybe get the bus to call round to collect her from the shop if George is... Look, is that Tom Kelso? Who's he in to see?'

Dr Kelso walks over towards the bed,

'Shirley, I was down in the city and I thought I'd call in, but I don't want to intrude.'

'Not at all, it'll be great for Maureen to have a wee bit of company when I get off home. I was talking about all the things

I need to do, so you sit down... How's Elizabeth and the boys? Well, they're not boys any more now, are they, but I... Well, time passes so quick.'

Shirley is self-conscious with Tom Kelso. He answers her calmly, as if she really wants to know.

'The boys are grand. David has a new car apparently. He's planning to drive them both over at Christmas.'

'Well, that's great. I'm going to head away on.' She turns to me. 'Make sure they phone if you need anything.' She then stoops and gives me a kiss. We're not a huggy family so it feels ominous, but perhaps it's for Tom Kelso's benefit.

There is stillness when she leaves. He smiles.

'Do you need some peace?'

I shake my head. A break from Shirley? Yes, but I don't want him to rush off.

'I've rung the hospital three times today. I don't care what they think. I needed to know you were okay.'

He sits with me. Silent. It's just what I need. I am so tired.

3

They introduce themselves over me. Two Smiths, Jane and Linda. No relation. I have time to listen as they wash me and make the bed.

"Do you think that's why Sister got us to work together?' says Linda, who has told me she is an agency nurse.

"We'll get called the Smiths. We'll lose our identity', says Jane, smiling.

Linda is about 45. A few babies have left tracks on her body, waisted dresses will always be tight now and she has the beginnings of lines round her mouth for lipstick to bleed into. She is kind and like the other agency nurses, works hard without grousing. She knows nothing of any of the other staff's backstory. She is fresh everywhere she goes.

Jane is a bright girl, probably has parents who think she should be a doctor, sporty looking but with hair that could tumble at any moment.

'So do you work part-time? Jane asks and then to me she says, 'Mrs McCormack, I'm just going to take your nightie off.'

"Yes, just a day at the weekend to keep my hand in. Roll this way dear,' says Linda.

"Is the pink nightie all right?' Jane is talking to me. I have trouble following this but luckily they use a special 'nurse' voice when they talk to me.

I nod a yes.

'I need to be at home for the children but their dad is around at the weekend. Are you local?' Then she puts the nursey tone back on, 'Now the good hand, Mrs McCormack, well done.'

'I'm from near Downpatrick.'

'Oh you're one of the Downpatrick Smiths?'

'Well, I suppose I am but there's a fair few families and we're not all related.'

'Do you know a Peter Smith, had a draper's shop in West Street, by the bridge?'

'Oh, I'm not one of those Smiths. I have a cousin round here in Antrim, runs a removals business.'

'No, rings no bells.'

'So do you have a big family connection?'

Now I know what she's trying to work out. Is she Catholic, did her mum have half a dozen brothers and sisters? This isn't as reliable as it used to be, as despite all the popes and bishops.

'I have two brothers and on the Smith side...' Jane counts on her fingers, 'there are about 8 cousins.'

It's inconclusive.

'So did you train here or across the water, Linda?'

'Manchester.'

'Did you like England?'

'Well you know Jane, you miss the family. I was glad to come back ... home.'

I can tell Jane was waiting for the 'Ireland' or 'Northern Ireland', but it's not forthcoming. 'There's no place like home, is there?' Jane looks at me. 'I'm sure you wish you were tucked up in your own wee bed, Mrs MacCormack.'

I smile and wonder when they'll find out each other's religion. I'm guessing Jane is an RC. She got told off for wearing a claddagh ring yesterday. It's not on her finger today. Linda is Protestant, just a hunch. She has a protestant way of folding things. I can say this because I am one. Linda runs her hand along each fold of the sheet with precision, making a little tent for my feet, resembling the Sydney opera house. She strokes my hand and then looks up.

'We'll be taking that drip out when the bag has finished, pet... So where will you work when you're qualified?'

'I fancy working in Dublin for a while.'

She's decided she's going to show her hand in this game or they'll get nowhere

'I hear it's lovely. I've never been down there. Never been down south at all.'

'Oh it's great crack in Dublin,' If I'm right, Jane would spell it craic.

So now they know, they're happy. It won't make any difference at all but they need to classify each other.

At the end of the shift they get me onto the chair for visiting and Linda watches as Jane disconnects the drip from my arm.

'Very good. Didn't feel a thing, did you Mrs Mac?'

*

I can see Jackie walking up the corridor, holding onto Shirley's arm. From a distance, they look a similar age. My sister seems oblivious to Jackie's unease, her watchful eyes snatching glances from left to right, like a little woodland creature fearful of predators. Jackie doesn't like new places. No matter where we planned to go, her first question would always be: 'Have we been there before?' And even if she couldn't remember visiting before, she would be reassured to know that it wasn't a new place.

After a while, I realised that what she was really asking was: 'Do they know me?' not 'Do I know them?' She needed to feel that the people and the place would be able to cope with her. In the end I would tell her that yes she had been there before, in order to reduce her anxiety, but Shirley didn't know all that.

'How's your sore throat, Mummy?' she asks now.

This was obviously Shirley's explanation for why I couldn't speak properly. I try to give an 'I'm okay' smile and croak out a yes which accidentally adds credence to the sore throat explanation.

'And you have a sore leg.'

'Yes.'

'Here.' She hands me a card, decorated with squares of paper and a chaos of small stamped patterns. She takes it straight back off me and then shows me the inside. There is a large, extremely neat letter J and by the time she got to K, her waning enthusiasm has made the letter formation rather relaxed. I blow a kiss, or at least I think I have.

'Do you like it?'

'Yes.'

Jackie turns to her Aunt Shirley.

'She likes it,' she says, triumphant. There has obviously been a bit of friction over the construction of this card. I smile, imagining the scene. Jackie and Shirley were never going to have an easy time getting on. Nothing to do with the Down's Syndrome – they are both as stubborn as each other and would have struggled to compromise even with the same number of chromosomes.

'Jackie made the card all by herself – would accept absolutely no help.' Shirley nods slowly, conveying her annoyance at this independence. It is not a compliment. No wonder Jackie looks chuffed.

'You're looking well,' says Shirley. 'There's a bit more colour in your cheeks but no wonder – it's powerful warm in here; outside it would skin you. Yes, you're looking better.'

Jackie is confused. 'You're better. Come on home,' she says.

Shirley reminds her about the sore throat and the sore leg.

Jackie wants to see proof. There is no bandage and no plaster. She doesn't trust us. 'Will you come home?'

'Yes,' I say. She is sitting on the bed and I try to hug her but she doesn't snuggle up to me and Jackie is normally a great one for hugs.

'She's been raging all day. I don't know what the matter is.' Shirley turns to Jackie. 'She'll be in here for a long time. She needs rest – away from you, young lady,'

23

Shirley is making it sound as if it is Jackie's fault I am in here! I shake my head and grab for Jackie's hand. Shirley is doing it all wrong. I want to correct her but all I can say is, 'Yes, yes, yes,' crossly. I start to cry and now Jackie is crying too.

Shirley drones on. 'I said it was a bad idea to bring her in. Now look what's happened.'

The nice nurse comes over with a tin of Quality Street. Jackie is making her selection and she has forgotten she ever had a mother.

'Don't go mad, Jackie,' says Shirley.

I want to tell Jackie to eat the whole box if she wants. I make a noise aimed towards the nurse and smile and nod.

'Are you sure you could manage one?' she asks, thinking I'm after a sweet.

I shake my head, still smiling, hoping she'll realise I'm trying to convey gratitude.

The nice nurse tells Jackie that I really miss her and I am trying my best to get better and to get home.

'I made a card,'

The nice nurse looks at the card and tells Jackie how much she likes the colours and that making your own card is a great thing for people in hospital because it shows you really care. She takes Jackie over to the desk and shows the card to the other nurses.

'She's a lovely girl,' says Shirley, nodding towards the nurse. She then lowers her voice. 'An RC, but lovely.'

For the love of God, Shirley, I want to say, it makes no difference what religion she is. I sometimes despair of my sister. If challenged, I know she would say she meant nothing by it, was just remarking... It does make me cross.

'You are tired. We'll head on before Jackie takes the hump again over something.'

It is true, I have found the half hour they have been here exhausting. Every emotion seems to wring the life out of me. I am glad Jackie came in. I hear the nurses talking about me but I do not have the stamina for eavesdropping.

4

A cheery porter sings in my ear as he pushes me out of the ward. No explanation, of course.

'We're off to see the wizard, the wonderful wizard of Oz.'

They have packed all my possessions into a large plastic bag. I must be being moved. A nurse comes running after us and tucks a big buff envelope behind my limp arm. At the ward door, we meet the Sister, who wishes me well. I catch sight of myself in a glass door while waiting for the lift. They shampooed my hair this morning and parted it on the wrong side. I look washed out in a pastel-blue velour dressing gown of Shirley's.

The lift takes me down to a waiting area and I am parked near big automatic doors; a red blanket is tucked round me. On a trolley nearby lies a young man in traction. I smile and then avert my eyes. I think he has a screw into his skull. But he's probably looking at me and wondering why I've got a lop-sided face. He is wheeled off and I am left watching the automatic door open and admit the world.

I am unexpectedly pleased to see a face I know from Derryconnor. This man used to drive Jackie's school bus and now he must work for the ambulance service. He holds on to the arms of my wheelchair and lowers himself down on his hunkers so we are almost face to face.

'Hello, Mrs Mac,' he says. 'I heard you were down here. I think we can squeeze you in – what do you think, Derek?'

Derek lifts my bag. 'You're our only customer, miss,' he says – and then I recognise him as one of my ex-pupils. No one else would call a fifty-something stroke victim 'miss'.

'Here's your limo, your ladyship. You let down the drawbridge, Derek.'

I doubt I could get a word in edgeways even if I had my speech. These two have the sort of double-act that men who work together seem to develop. I wish I could ask where we are going. There is a nurse in the ambulance too, but she is very quiet. We both look out of the window. A bleak mizzly rain starts and I hear the sound of the windscreen wipers going on. On a wall is written *We will never forseak the blue skies of are Ulster for the gray skies of an Irish Republic.*

Derek turns round. 'Standards of spelling have gone down since my day, haven't they, Mrs McCormack?'

We travel out of Belfast, towards home. Leaving the city, I realise that autumn is lost to me. Gone: a chunk of three or four months behind a forgotten combination number. I look at the winter changes with new irrational anxieties about dahlias not being lifted and Christmas shopping.

'Are you all right there? It'll be nice to get to the Infirmary. Easier for visitors.'

'Yes.'

Derek, the quieter ambulance man, turns round again to talk to me. So now I know. I'm being taken to the hospital local to home. Coming up to the roundabout outside Derryconnor, I hear the men talking. As the ambulance vehicle stops to give way, the driver calls back: 'Do you fancy a detour, Mrs McCormack? We'll take a spin past your house.'

'Don't let on to the boss,' says Derek.

I am trembling as the ambulance goes up the Drumana road and then along the side road up to the farm. I can see my sister's hand in the place. The curtains are all open and tied back to give symmetrical curves like a dolls' house. Very Protestant-looking, as they say. The dripping tap in the yard has been fixed and the dog's kennel must have been moved into one of the outhouses. I wish I could go straight in.

27

'You'll have to work hard at the old physio and get home soon, Mrs Mac. We don't want to be driving up here in the snow, do we, Derek?'

'Yes, yes,' I say.

I can hear them talking in the front, as if I can't understand when they don't put on their 'talking to patients' voice.

'Do you think she knows what she wants to say?'

'Oh aye,' says Derek. 'She's all there, so she is. You can see it in their eyes.'

The driver swings the ambulance round so it faces the slope near the lane leading up to the old spring house. We reverse out of the yard and drive towards Derryconnor Infirmary.

*

I remember one of the first times Tom Kelso visited the place. I had taken him to the spring house. It was before Jackie was born. He'd come to see my mother who was recovering from a fall. He was good with the old people and made them think he had all the time in the world. We got into a conversation about the water from the spring on our land.

'Do you want to try it?' I asked. And when he looked at his shoes: 'Come on. The ground's hard so you won't get muddy.'

I took my apron off and pulled on an old coat. I felt like taking his hand and running, because in winter it is a magical place and I had no one else to share the magic with. We walked past the stone-built outhouses with their red, turning-to-rust doors, then up the corrugated concrete slope. I lifted the gate to swing it towards me.

'Can I help?'

'It's a knack. It always sticks, but it's frozen today.'

Together we lifted, our breaths mixing in the icy air, grunting like sumo wrestlers. The metals of the gate and the catch snapped apart.

'Are you okay?' he asked as he put his hand on the shoulder of my old green tweed coat. I felt the warmth as though on my naked skin.

'Sure. We country girls are tough, you know,' and I suddenly saw myself as very bumpkin-ish, lumpy and red, clumping up the lane in slipped-on wellies and a heavy coat. A bit different from his wife with her pale skin and patent shoes. We reached the spring house and opened the rough door. It was sticking too. The water sprang from the back wall, which was part of the stony hill. Along the wall here were always drips from the porous rocks, small sparkles on a black background, like a dirty marcasite brooch. In other places, crystalline icicles poked like Christmas cake icing pulled into points with a knife.

'Oh. I forgot a cup,' I said.

'We can use our hands – you first.'

I rinsed my hands in the icy water, then shaped my already reddening fingers into a shallow cup and drank. I then reached under the flow again and splashed my face with the startling water.

As he bent down to drink, I said, 'It's always fresh even in summer but today it would make you gasp. Apparently old Father Toolis said this water was so pure it didn't need to be blessed.'

'Will it make me handsome?' he asked, smiling.

'I don't think you need that,' I said, feeling too daring already. 'Anyway, it hasn't worked for me yet.'

'Are you fishing for compliments?'

'Not *me*,'

He gathered some more water in the bowl of his hands and held it up. 'Another drink?'

I lapped it up like a kitten. When I had finished, he dried his hands on his jersey. He reached to wipe some water from my hair.

'You'll be covered in icicles.'

We stood in the spring house, surrounded by jewels and cold. Without speaking he opened the door and we walked back to the warmth of the farmhouse.

For years there were moments like this. Just moments, but they kept me going. There were never any moments with Walter.

*

Walter was a straightforward man. Genuine. Where I come from they'd say he had 'no side to him'. He never had a bad word to say about anyone. That's good up to a point, but he didn't say much at all. Walter liked plain food. He liked plain clothes. Some might say he liked plain women. He was pale with reddish, singed-looking hair. Where his face and arms got the sun, he was weathered. When he took his shirt off he looked as if he was still wearing a white T-shirt. He kept his hair very short. Any hint of a bounce in those ginger crinkles and he'd be down the barber's. As he got older, he pulled himself in tighter and became more rigid, mentally as well as in appearance.

Walter wasn't spontaneous. Walter didn't dance.

'Walter doesn't dance,' his sister would say. It was hard to get to talk to the girls if you didn't have that excuse. None of the boys were exactly Fred Astaire, but they made a stab at it to get their hands on a girl. Even that didn't tempt Walter. The dancing days were soon over anyway.

Walter always gave me money for my Christmas and birthday presents. He got his sister or Shirley to buy the cards. It was as if to choose something would be too much of a give-away. It would show what he thought of me. When he asked me to marry him, he looked at his watch first.

'I suppose we should get married soon,' he said, not even

meeting my eye. He could have as easily been suggesting it was time to do the milking. But he was a good man.

Of course things were all right between me and Walter, but nothing he did made me gasp or giggle. He was a good husband but we 'tried for a baby', we didn't 'make love' as the magazines were calling it. I think it was like that right from the start on his side. I got carried away with the idea of being married and didn't even notice his lack of enthusiasm. Serious Walter with his farm. He would stop you talking, mid-sentence, to listen to the weather forecast. Would he do the baling today, or could he risk leaving it until Monday? He was so pleased when I finally got pregnant. Sometimes I wonder if it was because he wouldn't have to turn that hug into baby-making. That's unfair. He was a shy man and I became shy too. Sex more or less stopped when I got pregnant.

We still shared a bed. Neither of us would ever have suggested otherwise, as that might have provoked a discussion. But in the summer Walter got too hot so I had to stay well away from him. In winter he didn't like a draught so he tucked the duvet down between us and the indent remained until the morning. There was never any trail of passionately discarded clothes up the stairs. I desperately wanted someone who put getting into bed with me before folding their clothes. Walter was always going to be a folder.

Yet he was kind in his way. He loved fixing things for me and we'd stay up half the night stretching canvases, or making stage sets for the school play. We worked well together, taking it in turns to get up during the lambing season. At night when it was my turn to check the lambing shed, he'd move to my side of the bed to keep it warm for when I came back. He would time the ram's visit so that the lambing would start a couple of days after the school holidays began so I could have a sleep during the day.

When he died, there was no one to bring me tea in the

morning, no one leaving the newspaper open with a big arrow in Biro pointing to an article I might be interested in, no one offering to clean the burnt saucepans or to run out in the rain to get the washing in. I only then began to realise there were other ways to measure the success of a marriage. The tea in the morning became symbolic. I thought no one would ever bring me tea in bed again. I didn't foresee the amount of tea I'd be getting in plastic beakers in a hospital bed.

*

We have arrived at Derryconnor Infirmary. I am pleased to be nearer home but part of me also wishes I could have kept hidden away. I am a vainer woman than I thought. The ward is the one my mother died in. It still has the sweet dry smell of floral talc that I thought was the smell of her but perhaps is the generic smell of female old age. The nurses are bulkier here and a bit older. Their uniforms look more like those worn by check-out assistants. Sadie, who I know from church, comes over to greet me.

'We've been expecting you, Mrs McCormack.'

For some reason this brings to mind a Bond villain and I cannot stop laughing and I can't explain why. She probably thinks I'm going senile, but she'll be used to that, as the ward is full of geriatrics. She ignores me while she studies the files of notes, the slim volume that has been tucked around me on the journey and the other thicker, more antique set of notes that chronicles my life: a tonsillectomy from when it was fashionable rather than necessary, a broken bone or two, a panic over appendicitis and later Jackie's birth.

There are gaps in there too, that few know about.

5

Walter and I had been married for about a year and a half when I started to get worried. There were jokes about the spring at first. It was supposed to help if you wanted babies. We bottle and sell the water now. It just about covers expenses but at that time people called round with bottles or covered pails and helped themselves. In those days you got married. You made sure your baby wasn't born for almost a year to give plenty of clearance to those who counted on their fingers to try to catch you out. After two years no baby came. Then my mother took me aside and asked me if there were any problems with our marital relations. I couldn't face old Dr Jones so when the new chap came in 1970 I knew I had put it off long enough.

That's when I met him. Tom Kelso.

When I walked in the room and saw him for the first time, I stopped at the door struggling to think of something else that was wrong with me. I did not want to talk about such things with him. He asked me about my cycle and talked reassuringly. He asked if I had ever been pregnant and I said no. I'd never had to deny it before. It's different from not telling. My face must have shown something. He hadn't even examined me.

'If there was something you didn't want to reach your notes, that would be all right.' He glanced at the doctor's notes. 'Maureen,' he put the stress on the second syllable – not like they do round here. Again I must have looked scared. 'It might help,' he said. So I told him about my first little baby, born in Glasgow in a home filled with scared Celtic girls.

'My husband doesn't know.'

'So it happened quite easily that time?'

33

'It was the first time.'

'Isn't that always the way?'

I wanted to tell him the whole story. I was blushing. I was a twenty-five-year-old married woman and I wanted to tell him the whole story to let him know that I wasn't that sort of girl.

'You were very young. Were there any complications, do you know?'

I shook my head.

'All normal then? Well, that's a good sign.'

I couldn't look at him and he must have seen that I was trembling.

'It's hard to keep secrets. Try to let it go. Are things going well between you and Mr '(there was a pause while he looked at the notes again) 'McCormack?'

'Yes, it's all all right,' I said, and I started making for the door before he asked me any more.

'This whole business is a bit hit and miss. See if you can relax, Mrs McCormack, and try to make love with your husband as often as you can. Come back and see me again. I'm sorry if this talk has upset you.'

I was out of the door and down the drive like a whippet.

*

I used to watch my pregnant colleagues at school, thinking there was no need for them to waddle in that 'just-about-to-drop' way. Barely five months gone and Stella Cochrane, Science Department, paraded the corridors, belly pushed out, hands resting on emerging bump, to taunt me. There was no need for this. I knew a thing or two about keeping a pregnancy quiet. Thrust your chest out, lean slightly forward when you walk, carry a big bag in front of you and try to proceed with grace. The staff room was full of them, it seemed: knitting and rubbing the small of their back, getting the best chairs and cups of tea poured for them. Discussions about varicose veins or where to get the best muslin squares surrounded me. Looking back on it, I wonder what was stronger. My desire to have a baby or me just wishing no one else would have one.

*

'You have a visitor.' Shirley rouses me gently.

I don't know how I sleep so much. It takes me a while to come round. It is Claire, my niece – Shirley's girl. She hugs me with abandon.

'Watch her. Go easy,' Shirley is doing some background fussing.

'I was in Sweden, filming a window-cleaner advert – in a light-house, of all things. I had to make a stab at speaking German and they'll dub it.' says Claire. She is studying me and sounding anxious despite her over-bubbliness. 'You've lost weight.' She fingers my wedding ring which they have secured with tape lest it slip off. 'How are things?'

I shrug and try to look grim.

'On a scale of one to ten, how are you – if one is near death's door and ten is Olympic athlete?'

I hold up two fingers.

'And how are you in yourself?' She curls two fingers of each hand to denote quotation marks for the 'in yourself'.

I put two fingers up and wave a third one tentatively.

'And the staff?'

I give them a seven to eight, though manoeuvring the dud hand is difficult.

'God, I couldn't believe it. Was it out of the blue?'

I nod.

'Bloody hell, you don't know what's round the corner, do you?

What's going to happen? You must be worried. All this worry and not being able to talk about it.' Claire rubs my hand gently.

'Don't get her all upset.' This is Shirley whispering.

'Oh, give over, Mum, for fuck's sake.' Claire becomes a teenager within two hours of being back in Shirley's locus.

'Claire!'

'If this is not a time to be serious, when is?'

Shirley decides to go to the hospital shop. Claire is dramatic, but then she is an actress. Sometimes it's hard to believe she and Maureen belong to the same species, never mind family.

'She must be driving you mad,' Claire says crossly. 'If you could be cured by fussing alone, you'd be up like a lilty.'

I smile, but I think she is being too hard on her mother today. Shirley is carrying a burden in the only way she knows.

'I love you, Auntie Maureen. You don't know how much. I know I'm over the top sometimes, but I mean it. I'd say this even if you were well, you know I would.'

If I were well, I'd probably be saying 'away on with you' or 'what are you after?' because like Shirley, I am uncomfortable with loving serious words. Talk of love slips more easily from Claire's lips, perhaps too easily, but today this is not theatrical luvvie talk. I wish I could tell her that I know she is sincere. I feel tears coming again and Claire doesn't try to stop them. She tells me it's okay to cry and I suspect that these are words she's seen in a script.

'I've never really seen you cry. I've seen you cross – with Granny and with Mum obviously, but mostly you're so calm with Jackie and everyone. I've never seen you cross with Jackie. There was one time... only one time when I thought you might be, but I couldn't work you out. It was that time you and Jackie came to visit me just after my twenty-first birthday. Remember when I lived in East London? You arrived all shaken and angry and yet

36

you wouldn't say why.' She pauses and then looks quizzical. 'Had Jackie played up? She was going through one of her "independent" stages and I remember her taking ages to do up her zip while we waited, coats on, boiling in the grotty hallway of my flat in Bethnal Green. You said nothing had happened but I knew something had. You were furious and upset. Not like yourself at all.'

Claire strokes my hand and then starts again.

'And Jackie seemed so young that time – so child-like, out of her usual environment. Not able to remember which door was the bathroom. Remember we had to put stickers on the doors? It was a good visit though, wasn't it? You relaxed after that first hour or so. I got that video out and Jackie watched it, reciting it word for word. Remember that?'

Yes, I remembered the film. Claire had been doing a lot of corporate videos. This particular film was for some small, now disappeared, Scottish-sounding airline. Claire played the passenger who didn't put her seat upright, she didn't fold her table away and she needed help with her seatbelt. She was the one who lit a cigarette, and she topped it all by tottering towards the safety chute in six-inch heels. In a real-life situation after all these mistakes, the stewardess would have cuffed her round the ear, not gently reminded her of the rules. Claire often sent us videos of her work for Jackie to watch. Somehow Claire's character seemed to always illustrate what *not* to do. In the careers video she turned up chewing gum. Jackie would tut at this bit. Claire's character was dressed in a short skirt and a low-cut top. 'This is not appropriate attire for a job interview,' Jackie would say, getting it in before the commentary.

I remember arriving at Claire's flat well. I wasn't cross with Jackie, as Claire had thought. On the journey over to Claire's, the frustration and fury at Jackie's condition had surfaced again, true – but mostly I was angry at myself.

To start with, Jackie was like any other baby. It wasn't until the other women, who had been in hospital at the same time as me, stopped pushing prams and walked along with their youngsters straining against their leather harnesses that it came to me: my baby and I were being left behind. I went back to work part-time and my mother had Jackie. Nowadays, Jackie might have got into an ordinary school but at that time it was out of the question. When she was six she got into the special school. A bus collected her from the end of the lane. Every morning we sat there in the car. The lane is almost a mile long so I'd drive to the bottom and then, when she was safely off, I went on to work.

On her first proper day at school, Dr Kelso came with a wooden pencil box with kittens painted on it. Jackie could still hardly pick up a pencil.

'Thank you,' I said when she was away. We stood and watched the maroon school bus with the wheelchair doors at the back head towards town.

'She thinks she's like Claire now, her cousin. I've told her it's not the same school, Doctor. What do I say? Do I tell her about Down's? Do I need to tell her? She's never asked. She doesn't see these things.'

'She'll know soon enough,' he said gently. 'You've made her feel special before she feels different. That's the important thing. You've done well, Maureen. Walter hasn't been able to help you much. You've been on your own.'

'Not quite on my own,' I said and smiled at him.

We were on the plane from Belfast on the way to London to see Claire, when I saw the moment Jackie finally realised that her mind hadn't really grown up with her body. She'd never flown before despite her familiarity with aeroplane safety instructions and I was scared she'd have problems with her ears. Down's Syndrome babies have endless ear infections. I still remembered rocking my sobbing child with her one red ear and flushed cheek. That day, although she was almost eighteen, I'd still stocked up on lollipops like the ones Kojak used to suck, in the hope of preventing any ear pain. I suppose I was still thinking of her as my baby. Perhaps the incident on the plane opened my eyes too.

After the initial excitement of the moment of take-off, when I had to hold Jackie's hand, I gave her the lollipop and helped her undo the sticky cellophane. Jackie was very pleased. She has a sweet tooth. The seatbelt signs went off and a little face looked at us over the top of the seat in front. The boy was about four. His little clear voice rang out over the dull hum of the plane.

'Look, Mummy, there's a grown-up lady eating a lolly.'

Jackie said nothing. The little boy bobbed down again, shushed by his mother. Jackie handed me the lollipop and said, 'I've had enough anyway.'

I could have cried. I felt I had set her up for ridicule. But Jackie's child-like ability to be distracted which has exasperated me over the years meant that the food trolley was enough to switch her uneasiness back to delight.

She was thrilled by the little cups and the plastic pack of cutlery, and I had to restrain her from going round the cabin asking for any unwanted mini-jars of marmalade. In the end the cabin crew gave her two full trays minus the hot breakfast in an airline carrier bag. That afternoon as she unpacked it for her cousin Claire to see, Jackie told us, 'When I grow up, I'm going to be an air hostess.'

Claire noticed my face fighting back a silent sob.

'You'll have to practise,' she said. 'You can start by learning how to make a decent cup of coffee for your mum.' Claire squeezed my hunched shoulders as she ushered Jackie into her kitchen.

Today Claire is hugging me again. She is still talking about the past,

'I used to feel guilty sometimes when Jackie asked me to take her places and I'd say no. Remember when she wanted to come to my eighteenth and you organised a mini-party for me so that she could be part of it? The twins came too, probably pushed into it by their father who always was a bit soft about Jackie – and you too, if I remember. But I wasn't too bad, was I? I did try to include her.'

'Yes,' I say, and wish I could say more because I have never really had a chance to tell her how much it meant to me. The truth is that although Claire has sometimes rebelled, she's been a saint really. When she was aged twelve, her father had had to pull her off a boy at the bus stop when she's overheard him making a nasty comment about Jackie. The eighteenth birthday was the only one Jackie had been excluded from because Claire wanted to celebrate adulthood with no family, no responsibilities and we understood.

6

I lie awake. A blade of yellow slides across my bed – escaping light from the gap in the curtains that encircle the bed opposite. It is three o'clock in the morning. There was some sort of crisis earlier: a death, a failing heart. Tomorrow the bed might be empty. They move the beds around here often; perhaps to try to shield us from the realities of death. So one day the person opposite, whom you have been cheerily waving to for a week, or the woman in the next bed who gave you a magazine, might be gone with no warning. Now that I can get about, I can sometimes find them again further up the ward.

It's not only the disruption that has kept me awake. As I get better I need less sleep. The inexplicably early morning tea and the strenuous physiotherapy is not exhausting me as it did at the start. This night I wonder about the future. Will I disappear in a bed reshuffle some morning? I am doing well but there are no guarantees. I have a vision of me still being here in years to come, very, very old and thin like the lady in the bed opposite. I have watched her struggling to drink and the Horlicks dripping from the side of her mouth and accumulating in the hollows at the bottom of her neck. Is that worse than my mother's stroke, which was followed by another and another and another – with no time to see any recovery in between?

Until now I have tried to keep unconnected my stroke and hers. She was old. I am young, only fifty-two. I have no place to 'pass on' to, so I am not worried about heaven or hell. There has been no temptation to seek out religion. But I want to have led a good life and I'm not sure I have, not even by my own standards. What are those Seven Deadly Sins again? I know that

envy is one of them and I have certainly been guilty of that –
and lust, of course. I've grown out of gluttony mainly because
of lack of time. My sins have been bitterness, regret, discontent-
ment and blame. I have been slow to feel joy – apart from with
Jackie. There were glimpses of it in the staff room, in the classroom and in those times with Tom Kelso, but I didn't look for it
enough. I didn't notice joy in my marriage. I didn't look for it in
the man who warmed my bed and worked my farm. I regret that
now. I was the talker. It was my responsibility to keep talking.
We could have learned about each other. After all, I would have
taken the time to learn about someone from Africa or Alaska. I
would have made allowances for differences in culture and dif-
ficulties in communication and prided myself in being
open-minded. But I didn't bother enough with Walter.

It wasn't just the marriage either. There was no reason to stop
painting. Lots of artists teach. Many teachers paint. I had to
have it all. And when Walter died? Did I sell the farm? Did I start
to paint? Did I travel? No. I worked harder. I took on teaching
a couple of evening classes. I took no holidays.

Walter hadn't stopped me. It was me all along.

*

Walter was working one day and dead the next. No sign of any
illness or slowing down. He finished the silage that day, moved
a few cattle and came in for his tea as usual. Jackie had made
cakes at the Centre. She tried to get him to have one but he
refused. He often did anyway, but this time he mentioned indigestion. I think it was the only time he ever complained about
an ailment, so I watched over him that evening. He was paler
and a bit slower than usual at moving around. I noticed him
slipping a Rennie between his lips but when I asked, he told me
to quit fussing.

In the morning he was still in bed when I woke. Even on our honeymoon he had got up well before me, so this was unusual.

'Are you all right?' I asked.

'That old indigestion hasn't shifted.'

'Not all night, surely? Why didn't you wake me?'

'Well, no point in us both lying awake.'

He looked the grey-white of street snow. I should have rung the surgery then and there. Instead we talked about what needed to be done that day and whether I could manage. I brought him tea. When I leaned to straighten the pillows, he squeezed my hand. I should have known then. He agreed to try a bit of porridge and I went downstairs to get it started. In the kitchen a wall of fear hit me. I moved the pot off the stove and ran straight back upstairs again. It was the squeeze of the hand more than the pallor that made me panic.

I came back to the bedroom with the cordless phone. I couldn't call 999 because a man who never touched me had squeezed my hand, could I? I called the surgery and asked for a doctor to call round. The lady doctor rang me back straight away. She knew Walter. Knew him from church, never as a patient. I described the chest pain and the paleness. I didn't have to mention the hand squeezing.

'I'll get an ambulance to you and I'll be there as soon as I can.'

I struggled to dress. I rang the McGoverns across the road and asked David to look over the animals for us. One sleeve in my cardigan, I telephoned Shirley to come for Jackie, still fast asleep in her bed. I looked for Walter's dressing gown and pulled the brush through my hair. I did everything but sit and talk to the man I'd shared a life with, the one time he would have been able to handle it. He more or less died in the ambulance, but they kept him hanging on until they got to hospital. He was only fifty.

What would he have said, I often wonder, in a deathbed

speech? I had not a clue what his worries were. I did not know what made him happy. We were a mystery to one another. It was such a sad day, but a bit like losing a parcel you hadn't even started to open yet. What if I had told him about the first baby right from the start? He was reserved and traditional, but I wonder now if he would have been all right about it. Perhaps if that big secret had been out of the bag, things would have been different. I know now that Walter wasn't totally to blame for the lukewarmness of our marriage. It does take two. I tried hard to start with, but when he wasn't the big passionate fellow I wanted, I packed it all in.

I never put my arms round him, never said I wanted him or that he looked good. Perhaps I did to start with – maybe not in a totally genuine way but because I was reading in *Cosmopolitan* that that's what you had to do. But it wasn't a *Cosmopolitan* relationship. He wasn't a *Cosmopolitan* man. So I stopped it all. The marriage was in some ways for me like a long slow huff. I never even talked about wanting things to change. Well, a hug you have to ask for isn't worth anything, so I didn't ask.

What would he have made of this: me being ill? I know he would have hated it. Hated me being ill, but also hated coming into the hospital to visit. Bedside scenes would have been as hesitant as bedroom scenes. He would have been saying he didn't want to tire me and disappearing if anyone else arrived. He would have immediately obeyed the bell signalling the end of visiting. He didn't like disarray and couldn't abide seeing me pottering around in my dressing gown even at the weekends.

'Is that you still in your disabells?' he'd say when he came in for coffee mid-morning.

And how would *I* have coped if *he'd* been ill for long? I think of myself as different but I'd have been as bad as him: running to the hospital shop, fussing over washing and choosing library books.

44

Tom Kelso walks in. He smiles at me from the ward door. He is more circumspect here in the local hospital. He will be known by most of the other patients, so there will be talk if he speaks to me but not them.

An old woman calls to him, 'Ah Doctor, did you hear about my hip? I'm after falling in the porch, last Friday.'

'Indeed I did. You'll have to keep off the sherry, Martha,' he says, obviously safe in the knowledge that she is no drinker.

'Augh, away on with you, Doctor, I was reaching for my letters and I heeled over.'

Dr Kelso goes over and has a chat, is shown bruises and directed towards her chart. I watch him. He is kind and patient and his smile twinkles over all those old biddies. I am jealous. He is never going to get to me. There is a very sick, elderly woman in the bed nearest to the nurses. I have never heard her speak, but he sees her and goes over. I can hear snatches of his side of the conversation but her voice is inaudible,

'... yes, terrible day. It's bucketing down but the forecast is good for the weekend. How are those grandsons of yours getting on?... Yes, I heard about that. Well, I'd better dander on, I thought I'd come over and see how you were doing.'

Oh, come and talk to me, I'm thinking. You have given those old women enough time.

At last he comes to me.

'I'm sorry. I didn't want to... I thought I should make sure I wasn't accused of favouritism.' He smiles at me and when our eyes meet, I still feel everything as strongly. 'Are you okay here? I rang Shirley. You sound as if you are doing well, getting more movement. It's great. You could make a full recovery.'

He pauses and rubs at a mark on his hand. He gives a small unnecessary cough.

'It's going to be hard to come and see you so often here with – you know. I would come twice a day but we have to see how things play out'. He pauses again. 'I have to think about Elizabeth.'

I don't know what to make of this. See how things play out? What does he mean? He looks nervous, flicking his eyes round everyone else in the room unconsciously before he rests his gaze on me again.

'I do love you, Maureen.' He allows himself one hand-squeeze. 'I don't know why we wasted so much time. I would not be able to carry on if you were gone. I'd leave anyway. Leave Elizabeth. Leave the whole shebang. I'm angry with Elizabeth and it is not her fault. She never made me marry her. She's a good woman. I just haven't loved her for a long time. And she knows it, I think. Actually I'm sure she does.'

I can't react because I have no voice but also I don't think I can process all this in my present state. I feel very tired. Tomorrow, will I know this wasn't a dream?

'You know my whole week used to revolve round you. When Jackie was a baby, I'd make you bring her in for check-ups she didn't need. The Health Visitors used to talk about Jackie getting special treatment. They used to tease me. I was like a young fellow. I liked it. Denied it, of course, but was pleased that someone else sort of noticed. It wasn't that I was enjoying the illicitness of it. It was never like that. I felt we were meant for each other. I was even glad when your mother had one of her falls. God forgive me, Maureen, I hate to admit it, but I was actively pleased to get bad news about that woman. It meant I could go out to the house and watch you move round your kitchen. I liked looking at you. When you reached up for the biscuit tin, your red shirt would untuck from your jeans to leave an inch or two of bare skin. I always accepted a biscuit, you'll remember.'

I did remember.

'No wonder that man is working all hours if he has a cup of tea with every patient he visits. Don't keep giving him tea,' my mother said one day when Dr Kelso had been to give her the injection for her anaemia. My mother didn't suspect she was getting any attention she didn't deserve, but she was suspicious of these visits. We'd stand in the yard chatting and when I came back in, Mother would be irritable.

'What were you talking to him about? Let the man get on for goodness sake, Maureen.'

I used to worry I was keeping him back, trying to keep the conversation going but he liked to talk to me. He wouldn't be here now if he didn't.

He came to me after Walter died. The undertakers were bringing the body home and he helped me clear a space for the coffin. It was the only time it felt wrong that he was there. I couldn't bear any reminder of how hopeless a wife I had been.

Tom talked to Jackie. He made *us* tea. He was a good friend to me then, like he always had been. He slipped in at the back of the church at the funeral and kept his distance at the wake. Afterwards he could tell I did not want to have any man about me. He did not come for a year and a day.

7

Shirley is always full of news and activity on her visits. Armed with newspaper cuttings, photos and magazines, she makes sure there is no silence despite my inability to speak. Even in the gaps she takes to draw breath, there is often the click of knitting needles. Today the news is that the Mothers' Union and the Ladies' Fellowship are to merge. This is big news, like hearing that Israel and Palestine are in talks. Elizabeth Kelso has been the chief negotiator.

That bit of news out of the way, Shirley works on the *Woman's Own* crossword, calling the clues at me.

'Fabric for ball gowns: something, something F something something something A. Oh, what is it?'

'Yes yes.' I'm really trying to speak. I inscribe a T on the blue bedspread.

'Tiff, Toff, Taff.' I am gesturing and nodding.

'Taffeta. Taffeta.' She gets it.

I nod and put my thumb up. We are laughing so much that the whole ward looks round. We continue as this weird dysfunctional charades team. Why have we never done stuff like this before? One clue stumps us both for a while.

'Bathed in a romantic glow.' Shirley thinks for a while, counting on her fingers. 'Rose-tinted? No, that won't fit. Nine letters. Come on, Maureen, you've always had a thing about romance. Remember all those films we used to watch?'

Yes,' I say and she is right, I always had a thing about romance. Candlelit, I am thinking but cannot say. Candlelit.

*

On our first anniversary I put a tablecloth on the table in the dining room we hardly used. We were living in the bungalow over by the low fields. I had reminded Walter about the date several times the week before. I wore a dark green princess line mini-dress with a bow under the bust-line. The dress had a black and gold fleck in it. If you drew your arm across it, it was scratchy. I worried it would catch my 15-denier tights and ladder them. I wore a hair-band and my hair flicked out, thanks to an afternoon in Shirley's heated rollers.

I made chicken Normandy to be served with rice which I had weighed out precisely. There were julienne carrots which I had prepared earlier. I had the wedding-present serving dishes warming on the rack above the cooker. I ran the Ewbank sweeper over the dining-room floor. The room was cold. This was before we had the central heating fitted in the bungalow. I brought the electric fire from the sitting room and plugged it in, hoping I'd be able to take the chill off the room, and then put the heater back without Walter noticing. Even at this stage in our marriage, I knew Walter wouldn't see the point of eating in the dining room when the kitchen was so much handier. On the centre of the table was the dark blue pottery candle-holder I had bought in a craft shop on the second day of our honeymoon. It was very modern. The matches lay on the table beside it, ready to light the candles for the romantic anniversary meal.

Walter came in from the redding up. He stripped off his dungarees in the back porch and walked into the kitchen in socks, still smelling faintly of straw and meal. I leaned to kiss him, not minding. I liked the maleness of him, just come in from the yard. He looked big and strong.

'I thought we'd have a bit of a celebration seeing it's our first anniversary.' I gave one of my smiles and raised my eyebrows in a way which I came to realise he couldn't read.

'I'll get cleaned up.'

'Do you like my dress?'

'Um, very nice.' I gave a twirl. 'There's not much *of* it.' He sounded disapproving, like a father, rather than a young man on his first wedding anniversary.

The candles lit, I sat waiting for my husband of one year.

'What are you doing, sitting here in the dark?' Walter flicked the main light on.

'I thought it would be more rom... A nice atmosphere.' He might as well have hit me.

'I won't be able to see what I'm eating.'

'Your eyes will get used to it. Don't worry, I'm not going to poison you.'

I tried not to show I was upset. I turned the main light off again and moved the table lamp to the edge of the side table. He liked the food but then he always liked his food as long as it wasn't 'too fancy'. The wine was nice, he said, but one glass was enough for him. I ate slowly, trying to make this into the sort of occasion it clearly wasn't. I talked about work. I asked him about the animals, whether he thought he'd get the potatoes in before the weekend or did he want a hand?

At ten to nine he started clearing up so he could watch the news. He was a helpful man. He respected my work in the house and always did his share when he could. I was the envy of Shirley, whose husband George would never do a hand's turn about the house.

'I thought maybe we could go to bed early, tonight.' I had swigged a third glass of Riesling by this stage.

'Go on up, if you're tired. I'll not be long.'

'I'm not tired.' I tried the smile but he was not looking. 'Oh, come up after the news,' I sighed.

Was he really so unaware or being deliberately difficult? I really never knew. I went upstairs, stripped off my dress and my silky slip and the posh wedding underwear and put on some thick pyjamas, buttoning them to the top to make a point. A point he never got.

A few days later, Shirley asked us about the meal. I had talked to her about what I had planned. I was glad George, Shirley's husband, wasn't there with his knowing looks and innuendos. It would have been too sad.

'Did you have a lovely anniversary meal?'

'Well, it was grand,' Walter told her, 'but Maureen had us sitting in the gloaming so I'm not sure what it was I ate.'

We all laughed.

*

'Are you okay?' says Shirley. 'Come on, we were having fun. Now you're off in a dream. Who succeeded Moses? Six letters, ends in A.'

I reach for the locker door. There is a small Bible tucked into a plastic bracket. But it's a Gideon Bible, New Testament only. The nurses tell her there is another Bible in the visitors' room. Perhaps those of us stuck in the ward are thought to be too fragile for an Old Testament God. Shirley comes back with it and starts reading about Moses. Pages and pages. Every so often she reads a section aloud.

'Listen to this. "And when ye reap the harvest of the land, thou shalt not make clean riddance of the corners of thy field when thou reapest, neither shalt thou gather any gleaning of thy harvest: thou shalt leave them unto the poor, and to the stranger". I don't think Walter read that bit, do you?'

I wonder at the detail in the Bible. How many would sign up if they knew all the small print? I tried to lead a good life even if I couldn't believe. I was well Sunday-schooled until about thirteen and then I fought with my parents about church-going every Sunday up until I left home. No stealing or killing, lots of honouring my father and mother though often with gritted teeth. I only occasionally took the Lord's name in vain. I did a fair amount of coveting and a smidgen of adultery. But I was reminded that 'The Ten Commandments are not a pick and mix counter,' as Shirley read aloud in an extract of Reverend Purdie's editorial in the church newsletter the other day.

'Joshua,' says Shirley now. I turn round, initially expecting to see someone of that name. She has had to read about three books of the Bible but is so pleased at getting the word. Shirley likes to finish things. She doesn't let things beat her. My being in here must be driving her mad. I expect her to leave now. I feel she has been here a long time. It is hard to focus at times. Shirley has done all she can in the crossword.

'I'll come back to it later. Sometimes if you have a break, the words come to you next time you go back to it.' She picks up the Bible and I watch her read. She looks like a devout Free Presbyterian at the bedside of a sick relative but I doubt if Shirley has ever read the Bible outside of school or church before.

'Some of it makes a lot of sense, so it does. Not the stoning people or an eye for an eye stuff, but Jesus was a good fella. You'd believe that even if you didn't believe all the other stuff.' Shirley flicks through a few more pages.

'But listen to this: Solomon's song – we never had this at Sunday school. "My beloved is white and ruddy, the chiefest among ten thousand. His head is the most fine gold, his locks are bushy and black as a raven. His eyes are the eyes of doves by the rivers of waters washed with milk and fitly set. His cheeks as a bed of spices, as sweet flowers: his lips like lilies, dropping sweet-smelling myrrh. His hands are as gold rings set with the beryl: his belly is as bright ivory overlaid with sapphires".'

Shirley tails off and continues reading silently. She has a good reading voice. I never would have thought it.

'A bit over the top, but isn't it lovely. George sometimes tries to get a bit poetic in cards but you can imagine his style. "Valentine, please be mine. I love you to bits 'cause you've got great tits".' We laughed and I imagined that was a censored version of George's 'poetry'. He was not the most refined of men.

'Did you and Walter still send Valentine's cards? Somehow I can't see him buying a card. We did a window display at the shop once, hearts and flowers, et cetera. I ordered in tea-towels with hearts on them. Walter called into the shop that day for a cup of tea. It was a Thursday. I tried to sell him one but he laughed and said, "She wouldn't appreciate me being all lovey-dovey." I thought that was a strange thing for him to say and told him I had always thought of you as being a bit soppy.' Shirley pauses and looks at me. 'No offence.'

'Then he got all serious. The shop was empty. He said you had been but the novelty had soon worn off and you were into babies and then Jackie came along and you had no time. He thought you had gone off him. I told him to talk to you, not to me – what did I know? He said he couldn't talk to you. All you talked about was Jackie or the school. I think he was scared of you, Maureen. He could talk to me because I was no threat but you... He adored you. You probably never noticed the way he looked at you as if you were some sort of unattainable creature who had had to settle for him. He didn't feel he deserved you. He thought you were the best thing that had ever happened to him. That's what he said: "Meeting her was the best thing that ever happened to me". But he said you had married him by mistake. I thought that was an odd thing to say. I feel bad telling you this now. I felt bad listening to him then. It came out of the blue. I didn't quiz him or anything. Should I have said something?'

I never thought Walter even noticed. We started the marriage with me feeling I was on the back foot, always terrified he would find out that I'd had the first baby. He had never had a serious girlfriend. Never had sex with anyone before me, I don't think.

Before the wedding we'd had a few adventures in the back of the car but he'd never seen me naked. There were faint stretch-marks on my lower belly, which to me shone in the moonlight. And that small jagged scar where I'd torn during childbirth, all healed but surely he'd be able to tell. I needn't have worried. He didn't look too closely. I never felt he cared much for my body. Physical affection did not come naturally to him and I didn't take that well. I felt rejected by him, so withdrew. It sounds like he then did the same. Perhaps we could have made it work even without the passion, if only we'd been able to speak.

'Sorry, I should keep my mouth shut,' says Shirley. 'I ramble on. I just meant to tell you that he cared about you even if he didn't always say. I don't know what happens to me sitting here talking to you. I open my mouth and don't know where to stop. You were a good wife to him. And you and he never rowed. Not like George and me. Good job I run a fancy goods shop, the amount of plates I've flung at that man. You and Walter were steadier. And it wasn't easy with Jackie. A sick wee baby. Well, they take over your life for a while. Look at the time! I'm away. Jackie will be back from the Centre if I'm not careful.'

Before she leaves, Shirley fusses around in my locker to get my laundry. She is always busy, never spending time on herself, through choice most of the time but perhaps now through necessity.

She looks pale and tired today. Shirley has a tendency to wear pastels which, even when new, look faded and drain colour from her face. She wears her hair long because George doesn't want her to get it cut. Today it is pulled back and clasped with a tortoiseshell device. It has started to soften and escape as she bends over to search for stray washing. She stands up impatiently and lets her hair down, tossing her head like a pony trying to avoid the halter. Then she quickly bunches it up again and stabs through it with the tortoiseshell dagger. Her reading glasses, worn on a chain, bounce off her bosoms when she walks around the bed.

Although not exactly fat, Shirley looks as if she was made in a bakery, constructed out of soft white bread rolls. She wears a matt powdery make-up which adds to the illusion that she is dusted with flour. There is often a lot of doughy cleavage on view. You can tell she is not totally comfortable with it. Today as she bends over to kiss me goodbye, she rests her hand over the V in her jumper as if reserving the view for George.

8

My baby, Jackie, I still think of her as that. I still think I have two babies. My first baby, my secret baby, has remained newborn in my mind and my second is trapped in childhood by Down's Syndrome. Try saying Down's Syndrome woman. It doesn't seem to fit, does it? Jackie's twenty-six now, an age when you have to stop describing her as a girl. It's hard to tell what age a Down's child is. There – I did it again. Most of them are short and have the unstretched face and loose mouth of a child, but before you know it they have acquired the comfortable pear shape of middle age.

I know a lot of Down's Syndrome people now, through the Day Centre and the parents' group. Other people find them hard to place. They are not used to reading their faces. It's like when white people say they can't tell black people apart. Probably we all look the same to black people too.

I'll tell you about the day my second baby was born. It was the day after my twenty sixth birthday. Shirley had dropped Claire's old pram round and I was trying the blankets in it when the labour started.

When the baby was born she was whisked away. Maybe that was normal for then. I got her back half an hour later. I didn't notice the eyes which are the main feature you think of. It's hard to tell with newborn babies. Their faces are puffy and their eyes look narrowed. The first thing I noticed, when I finally unfurled her from the tight swaddling, were the ears. Her tiny perfect ears like a china doll's were set low on her head. They looked unfinished, too delicate for a real baby.

I could hardly remember what a newborn baby felt like in

your arms. I examined her carefully. The back of her head felt flat, as if she had been moulded out of fondant icing and then put down on a flat surface to dry. I wondered why the midwives weren't more pleased for me. Had I moaned too much? Then I heard Walter outside talking with the doctor.

'No,' he said. At first it was as if he was refusing a cup of tea but then it grew louder and he was moved away. I wondered if they had made a mistake and were giving him someone else's bad news. Then I looked at my baby again. Her china-doll ears and her rag-doll floppiness. I felt so scared. Alone like a lost child myself. Where were the nurses? Where was Walter? Where was the doctor?

They all came in. The Sister nodded at Walter. He shook his head and walked out. The obstetrician came to me, sat on the bed and took my hands.

'Maureen,' he said, 'your baby's... not perfect. She's got Down's Syndrome. Do you know what that is? She's going to have a few problems. Your husband's a bit shocked.'

'Are you sure? She doesn't look...' and then I saw, superimposed over the baby's face like a Photofit, William Scott, the lad up the road. Brave little Billy Scott who sat in the corner at Sunday school and never said a word. Billy Scott who still got his dinner cut up for him aged twelve.

'You're right. I see it now. She's a Mongol, isn't she?'

There were no cards and flowers. No one looked at her. It was as if I'd had my appendix out. I got home two weeks later. The baby was to stay on in hospital for a couple of days. Everyone else took control. There was an assumption that I would have time to consider whether I wanted her home at all. I felt so depressed. I did everything they told me.

The baby's room was locked. I felt for the key in the fluffy dust on top of the architrave. The crib was made up though my mother had made no mention of it when I came home. She'd added yellow ribbons to hold the hood up. We'd planned on pink or blue depending on whether it was a girl or a boy. It seems silly now, but that's what you did then. Those yellow ribbons annoyed me. It was as if she thought of my less than perfect baby as an 'it'. We'd chosen the smallest room, a baby's room, cosy with a couple of rabbit pictures on the wall. A nursing chair stood in the corner, a crochet shawl hung over the back ready for the night feeds. Wood-effect lino covered the floor. I stood on it in my stockinged feet. It was cold, colder than real wood.

I slid open the drawers of the dressing table. They were full, little knitted cardigans and matinee jackets in one drawer and soft four-ply wool leggings and bootees in another. Where had it all come from? Then I realised. No one wraps presents for a less than perfect baby. It had all been handed to my mother when they'd heard the news with no pretty stork-with-baby paper or congratulatory cards. I could recognise my aunt's smocking on the little white nighties. I knew that my friend up the road had been crocheting that hat. I could picture Mother putting them in these drawers joylessly. The needlepoint sampler she'd been working on was left unfinished in the bottom drawer, together with the one my grandmother had made for my birth. Mine had *wrought by Anna Hammond* stitched along the bottom. Mum had already done the family name and even the year for the baby. The needle was left in the fabric. When she got the news she must have stopped and felt the birth wasn't worth recording.

On the top of a low trunk was a hemmed piece of yellow quilted plastic to lay the baby on to change her. Nappies and muslin squares were folded on the shelves like goods in a draper's shop.

Turning to the window, I pushed away the net curtains with the felty polka dots. Brushing a dead fly from the newly glossed wide window-sill, I sat down. Beside me was the regulation copy of Dr Spock and a book of babies' names. I looked up my baby's names. Jacqueline Anne after Jackie Kennedy and Princess Anne – well not really – they were popular names. It was hot on the window-sill but my feet were still cold from the lino. There were no frills, no cards and no toys in this room.

It was at that moment I decided I was going back for her. Jacqueline Anne would sleep in this room though she'd never be a princess or marry a president.

*

The only one that called was Dr Kelso. He brought me a card and flowers and a doll for Jackie.

'People sometimes forget you when it's not gone according to plan,' he said. 'I've no wee girl to buy dolls for. Here you are.'

I was leaning back against the range in the kitchen, hands rotating the silver rail that ran along its edge. I went faster and faster until it squeaked and then I turned to stir something.

'Talk to me, Maureen.'

'No. I can't start talking.' I stirred vigorously. The stuff in the pot had started to catch. I moved it to the edge of the stove. 'They don't want me to talk. They all want to pretend nothing has happened. To them she's not a baby. She's like a runty lamb brought in a cardboard box and left in the corner of the kitchen to see if she'll make it.'

'Who's them?'

'Walter, Mother, Shirley, everyone.'

'Where is she?'

'Mother – she's doing the messages. Walter took her in. They don't even want me to go out.'

'I meant Jackie.'

'She's in the hall, in her pram. My mother says it's too hot in here for her to sleep. They don't want to have to look at her.'

The hall was dark with furniture. The pram looked like it was being stored there. He pulled it almost angrily into the kitchen, scraping the brake lever against the door and ruching up a strip of paint. Jackie's fine brown hair was damply spiked to one side. He rubbed it down and stroked her face.

'Feel her skin. It's so soft. They don't stay like that for long.' He took my hand and held it to Jackie's face. I bent down into the big carriage pram and put my cheek to hers.

'Nobody else has said anything good about her. I think she's beautiful.'

Jackie's little hands clenched and unclenched. Then I couldn't speak. The pain came. The pain that for days now had taken hold of my upper torso when I struggled to keep control. A giant claw reached into my chest and lifted a fistful of me. The pain spread numbingly down my arms. To anyone else it would have appeared a physical symptom. A heart attack maybe?

'I've lost my baby. This isn't the baby I was carrying in my dreams. I feel I've lost a second baby. But look at this wee help-less thing. How could I not love her? But she isn't the baby I thought...'

Another wave of pain and I couldn't get the air into my lungs. He held my shoulders and I could hear the sound as he pulled the kitchen chair in behind me and lowered me onto it.

I howled like a child after a bad fall. When I calmed down, the agony in my chest had lessened and the closing up of my throat had eased. He was crouched down by my chair and I was crying into his chest. He held me tightly to him. His hand was cupped round the back of my head like the way I had to hold Jackie. Gradually I started to relax and was conscious that my nose was wiping on his jersey. I got up.

'Sorry, you daren't give me any sympathy or you start me off like that.'

'You could do with a bit more sympathy. Will they be home soon?'

'God, the dinner.' I started stirring again.

I put the pot on a stand on the table and contrary to my mother's instructions, I lifted my sleeping baby for no reason but my own need. Neither Walter nor Shirley nor Mother had laid a hand on me since I came home. Even little Claire, who was normally all over me, trying to plait my hair or asking for a piggy back, had been kept away. I hadn't thought that my own child could comfort me but she did. I carried her round like a security blanket with my mother muttering that I was making a rod for my own back.

I used to walk for miles, in those weeks and months after Jackie was born. In those days people did walk more – but not if they had a car. Walking as a pleasure is not something people in the country do. My mother thought I was mad. Perhaps she was right? I pushed faster and faster until I could have passed a jogger. These days, people have those three-wheeled buggies, but this was a big sprung Silver Cross pram and I was in court shoes. There was a lot of political trouble at the time. It was the tail end of the marching season and I could sometimes hear bands in the background. Derryconnor Pride of Ulster flute band practised at the Orange Hall at the end of the road up to Ballinstavey. Internment had just started and on the main roads there were lorryfuls of soldiers passing, heavy guns resting non-chalantly in their open hands. They used to wolf-whistle me and shout, 'Cheer up love, it might never happen!' in their chirpy English accents.

I'd end up somewhere and not remember any of the journey. 'The road runner', Shirley's husband used to call me. Mother said people were laughing at me. No: 'Are you depressed?' No: 'I can't bear to see you in so much pain', just: 'What would the neighbours say?'

I got no pleasure from it. One day I walked twenty miles. My feet were bleeding. I had used up all the bottles at the foot of the pram. Trying to buy a bottle of milk in a shop, I found I had no purse on me. The woman behind the counter had a brown apron on with gingham trimmings. She had the complexion of someone who had been out in the wind for too long. She didn't want to give me the milk when she found I had no money, though she could see I was desperate. I think she thought I was a gypsy and that she'd start something. They'd all be in for milk on tick for crying weans – that was her thinking. I sat down in the shop. In those days, shops had seats where old women would sit while someone else ran and got their shopping. My legs were splashed and I had a pull in my stockings.

Jackie kept on crying. I didn't even know where I was. Eventually the shop woman started to lift Jackie and then she let her back down – not quite dropped her, but she would have, if she'd let her instincts take over. She lifted the milk from the counter and took the bottle which was poking up from under the pram cover.

'I'll scald the bottle and warm it up for you,' she said. There was still no kindness in her voice. She came back from behind the counter and sent a boy out the front. He didn't look like he'd had much experience of her maternal love. The boy came back, out of breath and pleased with himself, cheeks red from the wind. He'd end up with her face too.

'He's coming.'

I was confused. I needed the toilet. Apart from the milk, there had been no other conversation. How could she know who to send for?

A fat old priest came in the door. I waited for him to ask for some tobacco or enquire after a relative but the shop woman nodded towards me. It was for him the boy had gone running. The priest had comb marks on one side of his head and the other side of his hair was blown over by the wind. There was that priestly frost of dandruff on his shoulders, that build-up accumulated by men who live alone and walk out the door not looking anywhere near a mirror. He put a hand on my shoulder but still faced the shop woman. Jackie was asleep on my other shoulder.

'Do you think she's taken the baby?' he said quietly.

'Look at it.' The shop woman tried to mouth it, but I could hear. I knew what she meant. The priest put his hand on Jackie's head and she turned to look at him.

'What a lovely babby,' he said too enthusiastically. I later came to value even those sorts of forced compliments for my child, but I seethed. He turned to the woman. 'Where's she from?'

'Not from round here,' she said as if he'd know it, as if there were two places in the world, 'round here' and 'not round here'. 'Can you take her home?'

'Don't worry, I'll walk. I'm all right walking. If I could use your toilet... ?'

The shop woman called the boy who took me round to an outside toilet. He stood waiting, kicking stones against a church-yard wall, as if he too sensed I was too unpredictable to leave. The pair in the shop had obviously had some sort of case conference, and by the time I returned, it had been decided that the priest would take me home – to whatever part of 'not from round here' I came from.

In the chapel hall car park, the priest and the boy started trying to dismantle the pram with me just watching. A wee boy and a celibate man struggling with something I could do in seconds. I got into the back of the car, my dress wet from the leaking nappy but I didn't apologise or explain. Paudric, the boy, sat in the front, a chaperone for this mad Protestant woman. They must have known I was not one of them or I would have reacted differently to the sight of a priest no matter how exhausted I was.

I told them where I was from and the priest humphed and turned back to get more diesel for the car.

'Did ya get the bus here, missus?' said the boy. 'Did ya get lost?' Why did ya come to Creggantoy?'

'Leave her,' said the priest. 'Leave her be. She's tired.'

I had told him where I needed to be dropped off in relation to the local chapel and public house. I had chosen the landmarks well and he needed no more directions. We sat in silence.

'This'll do. This'll do. Stop here.' I began to panic. 'This is grand. Just leave me here. I'm so grateful.'

He dropped me well away from our lane, in the car park of a disused Orange Hall. I couldn't face the talk from Walter and Mother if a strange man had brought me home. And a priest!

'Imagine! A priest. She had to get brought back by some priest,' they'd be saying and Shirley and Shirley's husband would have to be told.

'Why did you go away there?' they'd say.

'How far would that be, Walter?' someone would ask, and Walter would get the map out and a bit of thread and they'd be asking what roads I took.

'Show them your feet, Maureen,' Mother would say. 'Do you see her feet? Would you look what she's done to her feet?'

So I told no one, but it scared me and I started to question myself as I got on with my life. Is this what a normal person would do? It was as if I was acting and deciding what my character would do, how would they react and what would they say? I was a mad person playing the part of a normal person; the opposite of Olivier playing Lear.

A fortnight later I was still wearing Walter's slippers, my feet were that cut up. I took the car and said that I was going to the doctor's. I left Jackie with Mother and drove to see the priest again. The chapel and the parochial house were a good half a mile down the road from the VG shop. I knocked on the house door, still in men's slippers with the backs folded down. He wasn't there. I went to the chapel door. I could hardly go in. He hadn't wanted to help me then. What could he do for me now? A Catholic church. Were Protestants allowed in? Did you still have to cover your head? Should I try to cross myself? I was still in the porch when he came out.

'I came to thank you for the lift.'

'No problem. No problem at all.' He made it sound as if it was his catchphrase.

'I'm a Protestant.'

'I'm allowed to give lifts to Protestants.'

'I meant I'm not one of yours.'

'Are you better now?'

I told him everything. I was there for an hour and a half. I know he was trying to stop me but I went on and on regardless. The first baby and the memory of spraying breast milk across the dark heavy furniture of the mother and baby home as they bound my breasts, the marriage and how Walter never hugged me, my childhood, the day I got pushed in the nettles, the misery I felt now. All the sad and bad things that had ever happened to me. I don't know what I wanted or expected. Some sort of solution or absolution. Perhaps if I'd been one of them, an RC, I would have got a different response, but he basically told me, that's life and you've got to endure it. No mention of God. Not unsympathetic but powerless. Perhaps for a Protestant, he didn't feel he had to come up with a formula, three Hail Mary's or whatever and away you go. Was this an inferior service or a more truthful one than usual?

*

The worst part of being stuck in this place is the hospital chaplain; I can see him approaching now. Sneaking in at the end of visiting, Reverend Kum Ba Ya, they call him. He's the curate of a church in a village outside Derryconnor. I never believed (though that's not really an option here) but now I'm powerless. He holds my hand and prays for me to find strength to do my exercises. He prays for my family who have to cope without me. He prays for the physio, the nurses, the doctors and the porter as he spots one out of the corner of his supposedly closed eyes. What about the cleaners? I want to say. What about the fellas who work in the morgue?

'Do you find comfort in prayer, Maureen?'

'Yes,' I say weakly several times. Some response, even if diametrically opposed to what I really mean, seems better than letting him fill the space with his own talk. He has those pious looking-to-heaven eyes and he holds his head to one side as if permanently questioning. He is sitting on my bed and the tucked-in covers are even tighter. I want to un-tuck everything and kick my legs out and tell him to leave me alone. I am so cross I can't even pretend to fall asleep which I have found is a useful way of getting rid of people. I stare at him with hatred. Insensitive as he is and inexpressive as I am, he gets the message and stands up to move on.

'Remember, Maureen, you are never alone.'

'Yes,' I say, though I disagree.

*

I start thinking about how alone I actually felt back then. About how the Creggantoy priest and Tom Kelso were the only people I could talk to in those years after Jackie was born. I think of Jackie's first birthday. I had made a little cake. We were waiting for Walter to come in for his tea. He said I was wasting my time. No one year old knew what a birthday was, but especially not Jackie.

Then there was a toot in the yard. Dr Kelso had his two boys with him and he brought them in. They were dressed immaculately in navy cardigans and grey trousers. I felt they were looking at me and my house and thinking how different I was to their mother. He brought a rattly ball for Jackie. The boys opened it for her and threw it back and forth in front of her. She was slow to pick up where the sounds came from and she looked as if she was watching Wimbledon in slow motion.

He told me they had a new doctor starting at the practice. He tried to slip it into the conversation but I knew at once it had been placed there for a purpose.

'She's a lady doctor, Maureen. I think you'd be better with her. You know, when you're having a family.'

'But I've had Jackie now. I don't need to change.' Then I realised he wanted me to go off his list.

'She's very nice. I think she'd be better for a young mum like yourself.'

I was so hurt. There were tears in my eyes. He knew I was falling in love with him. He thought I was going to cause trouble.

'Well boys, what about some cake?' I said.

'We wouldn't want to intrude,' Dr Kelso said.

'There's nothing to intrude upon,' I snapped aggressively. 'Absolutely nothing.'

I lit the candle with a bit of screwed-up paper from the fire. Some sooty flakes fell on the cake but they disappeared when the boys blew the candle out for Jackie. I cut the cake and handed it out abruptly. Walter came in. For all his talk I could see that he was hurt that I hadn't waited for him. I was glad. I hated the pair of them for their diffidence or indifference. I put the tea-pot on the table, pretended to smell Jackie's nappy and took her off to change her.

9

It was high tea on Sunday at my sister's and grace had just finished. We always said grace if my mother was there. I wonder did she know it didn't happen all the time. Gammon and pineapple juice dribbled over the white tablecloth and my mother fussed over it while I mashed up Jackie's food. Walter and my brother-in-law were talking about cars. My sister was telling me what had happened in *Crossroads* on Friday. Claire, then about aged seven, was silent. I had watched her quizzical little face listening to grown-up talk all afternoon. She was a bright wee thing. I had taught children like her and they were a joy.

My mother had made pavlova, her speciality. We had pavlova or lemon meringue pie every Sunday afternoon. Claire cadged some extra strawberries off her father. Silence followed as they all crunched their spoons through the meringue. I smiled at Claire as she looked over. I was still spoon-feeding Jackie even though she was four. Claire focused her gaze on me again. I thought she was after some of my dessert.

'Jane Ferguson says that Jackie is Doctor Kelso's baby.'

If I had been eating I would have choked. It felt as if everyone had dropped their spoons and frozen. My mother was the sort of person who didn't gossip. Real horror showed on her face. She was furious but I could see her push that fury down as if it was a physical effort.

'What a story,' she said lightly. 'Uncle Walter is Jackie's daddy. He's married to Jackie's mummy.'

'But Jane's mum...'

'I'm sure you'd like more pudding, dear.' It sounded like a threat. 'Come into the pantry with your plate.' Mother took

Claire's arm and marched her through the kitchen. If there hadn't been complete silence in the dining room we wouldn't have heard anything. All we heard were snatches. My mother had changed from that nice gentle pavlova-making granny to the scary mammy of my childhood.

'If I ever, ever hear...' You could tell that Claire was mystified.

Then Jackie was sick, my little saviour. I went to the bathroom to clean us up. My sister followed me with the changing bag.

'What a story,' she said.

'Kids,' I tutted, not looking up.

'You should watch it.'

'It's not true. '

'Maybe you want it to be.'

'Oh for God's sake, Jackie's not been a well baby. I've needed a lot of help.'

'Maybe you should have been getting some of it from Walter.'

'Yes, maybe I should. Or from you' I said.

And yet this wasn't totally fair. I had turned from her as much as she had turned from me. We went on to have a row and I accused Claire, little Claire who was only seven, of deliberately trying to cause trouble. And Shirley accused me of being bitter and jealous because she had a normal daughter. Characteristically, there were no apologies or any attempt at discussion at any time later. We just stepped back farther and farther from each other when we should have been sticking together, protecting each other from Mother and her fussing and harshness.

*

Shirley and I were as thick as thieves when we were younger. There was no point in being a clype because even if we told on each other, our mother's wrath fell evenly on both the 'victim' and the accused. Listening to us was a bother to our mother. She had cows to get in and hens to feed and endless black-leading of the stove to do. I can't picture her as a character in our childhood without either her apron or coat on. In old photographs I see dresses I only recognise from the ironing board or as soft flowers flapping in the wind on the washing line. These dresses appear on my mother as unnatural as the clothes on a paper doll.

My mother was concerned with how things would look, not how things were. We had to wear a cardigan not because we were cold but because otherwise it would look as if our mother didn't care. We weren't allowed to wear our school shoes on Sundays even when the Sunday shoes got too tight. Shirley and I cut each other's hair once. We used Mother's sewing scissors and a series of mirrors so we could show each other the styling at the back. We had been playing 'beauty parlour' and wore towels turbaned round our heads, dolloped Pond's cold cream onto our faces and rubbed red Smarties over one another's lips. Then we started on the hair. Shirley's finished hairstyle was quirkily asymmetrical but still shoulder-length in places. I ended up with tufts and hollows and a bald section at the back.

Our quietness had made Mother suspicious and she burst into our salon in the cupboard under the stairs. She grabbed both of us so hard I had the sensation of a Chinese burn in my armpit and stood us at the hall mirror.

'Look – look in the glass. Look what you've done. How can I show my face outside this house? You'll be the talk of the country. For pity's sake, you look as if you have been in Buchenwald, Maureen.'

My mother sounded as if she thought it would have been better for me to have been in a concentration camp than for her to have to explain what had happened. She locked us in the meal-house all day and we had to pee in a bucket and drink from the dirty old tap used for adding water to the animal feed. At five our father came into to the meal-house and discovered us. He sent us inside.

'Go and tell your mammy you're sorry.'

In the house, Mother was polishing the parquet floor in the hall. Sorry wasn't enough. She wanted to know whose idea it had been.

'It was both of us.'

'At the same time.'

Mother put me in the spare bedroom and Shirley in the dining room. They were both cold formal rooms with no toys or books or distractions. We were told where to sit and warned not to move. She interrogated us individually. No nice cop, just nasty. I could hear her shouty infuriated whisper as she went on and on at Shirley. She couldn't bring herself to shout, even though we were miles from any other houses.

She thumped up the stairs to start on me. I sat on the cold green satin eiderdown, slipping off the high bed from time to time.

'Sit still and listen. I am so disappointed in you. You tell me who started this whole caper. I just want the truth and then we can forget about it.'

I knew that there would be no forgetting in this house today so I kept quiet.

'I do my best – and look at you. You look like a wee girl riddled with lice.'

And finally, the ultimate threat.

'I don't want a wicked girl in my house. You're the oldest. If you don't tell me who started this you'll be sent to Barnardo's. Tomorrow. I'll start packing now and there'll be no toys going with you.' She reached for the suitcase on top of the wardrobe.

'Can Shirley come too?' I asked in a small hopeful voice.

She hit me a clout that threw me back onto the green shiny

bed. She had lost control and I was scared. She had shocked even herself and I could see her face redden and she glanced in the mirror. She came towards me again, probably to check for a mark on my face but I ran out the door and down to get Shirley. On the way out I lifted a whole sponge cake, cooling on the rack in the kitchen. I carried it in the skirt of my dress as we ran across the yard and up to the spring-house in fear of our lives.

Of course that's an exaggeration. We were in no danger. Mother was scary and strict but she loved us. Most of the time we stayed out of the way. When called in to help we had a game where we would pretend to be in service in a great house. 'Little servant girls' we called it. Mother ignored or didn't notice our curtseys and 'yes ma'ams'. Together we weathered and even enjoyed life in that rather rigid house sustained by paper bags of boiled sweets brought home by our dad on the days he went to the mart. In the spring house that day though, we were fearful. We knew we had gone too far.

'It was only meant to be a trim,' I said.

'I'm a beginner.' Shirley was apologetic. Even she could see I had come off worst.

My father was sent for us an hour or so later.

'Come on in. It's over now, so it is. She was just worried. You could have cut yourselves. That's all.'

Shirley and I held hands and stood firm.

'I promise you it's over. I'm finished the redding up. I'll be in the house.'

My father took us each by the hand and walked us down to the house. As we got to the yard, he stopped.

'Not a peep out of you. Your mammy has a headache.'

The next day we had the morning off school. Mother took us to the hairdressers. Not Sharon's, where she got her perm, but we had to go to the one owned by a Catholic lady at the bottom of the town because she was 'that affronted'.

'I'll have to give her a boy's cut,' said the Catholic lady. 'There's not much left.'

'Just do what you can,' said Mother, bleakly.

I watched as I got transformed into a little lad. A couple of tears ran down my face and the fine trimmings of hair stuck to the damp like stubble. The hairdresser ruffled what was left on my head, sparse and mousey where yesterday there had been long waves. It wasn't even long enough to shade it into a side parting.

'It'll grow really quick. Don't fret, darlin'.'

By the time it came to Shirley's turn, my mother had gone round the corner to get some messages.

'What will I do with yours, love?' the hairdresser asked.

'I'm having the same, the exact same as my sister.'

That summer we wore shorts and pretended we were little footmen silently following orders from our cruel mistress.

*

When did it start? The moving away, the different lives, the withholding, the not asking, not telling. Shirley seemed to become one of the enemy rather than my ally. I think my mother had drummed 'keeping yourself to yourself' into us so well that each of us ended up not even talking to our own sister. Let's think back... The haircut must have been when we were four and six. At seven I still sat with her on the school bus. We wore identical green pinafores with rows of red rickrack at the bottom to disguise the fact that they'd been let down. I hit a boy who said she dribbled. At eight I went to the Girl's Brigade and she cried because she couldn't get in. At nine she started the piano and came back on her own from town. I didn't want to have her at my tenth birthday because of a fight about some paint she'd spilled, but relented at the last moment. Shirley was eleven when she took some nail varnish of mine. My mother had asked who brought the tools of harlotry into her house. We were whores, according to my mother. Two little girls with bitten nails, hands stained with fountain pen ink and the ends of our fingers, dabbed clumsily with crimson.

'It's Maureen's,' she said. 'She let me borrow it.'

My mother had finally won. She had divided us. We were broken. When I went to Scotland to have the first baby, I was sworn to secrecy. It was as if the one big secret made it impossible to share anything in case it came out. My mother was full of 'If this gets out...' threats which put a stop to any interaction. Perhaps we would have reconnected after motherhood but my Jackie then became the un-discussable subject.

But today as Shirley sits with me beside my hospital bed, I feel we are as united as we once were. I am full of her secrets and would tell her mine if I could. This has opened things. I have become everyone's confidante – but will they regret it when I get better? I am thinking this is temporary but I assume they believe it's permanent otherwise they wouldn't dare confide. Today I made big progress in speech therapy: doing counting, the alphabet (only up to M for some reason), the months and days, that's all. It's a struggle and I worry it is automatic talk, like a reflex. I haven't missed talking, which is strange for I loved to chat. Now I feel I used it to stop rather than start communication. The speech therapist is pleased with me. I imagine her at home having her tea with her family. I see her fork plunging into a chicken Kiev because she is rounded, buttery and always smells of garlic.

'My wee stroke lady has got some new words,' she'll be saying. 'You know, the one who could only say yes.'

'What did she say?' The children will be excited.

And they will be disappointed with one, two, three and January, February, March. They will want secrets and truths. I could see her delight today. So patient, so enthusiastic all along, she clapped like a little girl. 'Your family will be powerful pleased.'

I put my finger to my lips and made a noise related to but not exactly a 'shh'. I will bide my time.

The Ward Sister is on holiday this week. No frilly cap to put the fear of God in the rest of the staff. One of the auxiliaries, a lazy wee thing, is showing a new student nurse round.

'You're supposed to top and tail them every night but if you get stuck for time I'd leave the ones that can't talk, like her. But I usually wet the cloths, in case Sister checks.'

Disillusionment in a fresh face is hard to watch.

'I'll do her tonight, will I?" says the student nurse and she turns to me with a smile. 'Is that okay?'

'Go on ahead.' The auxiliary drops her voice but not enough, 'She was a teacher. She taught me. Her name's Maureen, poor creature.'

I remember her then. A defiant little girl with dark hair who curled her lip when you told her off. Now she's ash blonde with a yellow uniform tight across her hips and muscular legs in black tights.

'And what about the patient in bed thirty-one?' says Jeanette as I now remember is her name.

'I don't smoke,' says the student. Going to the patient in bed thirty-one is code for going for a smoke. There are only thirty beds here. Even I have worked this out. The student (I can't read the name on her badge, because her pens are sticking out of her pocket and obscuring it) goes to get a basin of water and swishes the curtains round. She pulls the bed table up towards me, wets the cloth and turns to me.

'Soap on your face?'

'Yes,' I said. Well, what else? She rubs the soap against the white 'J-cloth' and hands it to me. She was going to let me do it

75

myself. Usually they give you a cat's lick like a mother with a hankie before a family photograph. She put it into my 'good' hand. I rubbed at my face and neck not quite knowing where I was reaching for. The soap smelled like doctor's hands. Rinsing the cloth and handing it back, she smiled.

'It's *Mrs* McCormack, isn't it?'

'Yes'.

'I'm not from this part of the world. It must be strange knowing your nurses.'

Later, she produced the green cloth for washing 'possible' 'I'll wash down as far as possible, then up as far as possible and then you can wash "possible",' they'd say when they were doing bed-baths. Hospital jokes – I've heard them all.

'I prefer working on my own,' she rambles on. 'You can do things at your own pace. There's no need for all this rushing half the time.'

The trolley comes round and I get Horlicks. I'm drinking it now. I like the chewy bits on the bottom which I can just reach if I suck hard enough with this straw. They are settling me down for the night now. They put a pillow at my back the way I used to put a rolled-up blanket behind Jackie. They pull my arm and leg out to prevent them snapping back like chicken wings. The student is even spreading my fingers like the physio does so they don't fall into an old woman's claw.

'Sweet dreams,' she says like a little mother.

'Yes.' I am smiling my lop-sided smile.

10

'I have money. If it comes to money, I have plenty.'

This shocks me because Shirley's husband George is always saying that the shop hardly covers their wages. I must look sceptical, because Shirley goes on.

'Honestly. I've been putting away money for years. It's there for any emergencies or Claire getting married or something like this. I have eighty-nine thousand, sitting there in a bank in Belfast. And I have cash coming up to another four thousand now. It's tucked into a section of my jewellery box.'

I shake my head to convey disbelief. She is already talking quietly but now her voice drops to a whisper.

'George doesn't know. I lift it from the till. He's hopeless at maths. He thinks we're just ticking over. If we seem to have a good month, I buy myself things and show him. It pleases him but then I take them back to the shop and bank the money.'

Things start to make sense now. Shirley is never in anything new but George is always talking about the big spender she is.

'I do it because I don't trust George.'

Shirley has always seemed to be too indulgent with George. He is the sort of man who'll come up behind you and give a playful slap on the rear end or put his hand on your leg when he has an audience and try to slip it up your skirt when he hasn't, knowing full well he'll be stopped. It's harmless fun to him, meant to embarrass me – and he does it to Shirley too. Ruffling her hair, pulling her onto his knee, talking about melons or bazookas or bonking. There is the air of the *Carry On* film rather than any passion or sensuality in the way he behaves. All talk, I assumed.

George knows all the women in town. The shop was his family business. Shirley was a Saturday girl there while she was doing her secretarial course at the Tech. She went on to help with the books even after she got a good job in the solicitors. She knew what George was like before they got together. A wolf-whistler, a slap and tickler, more Benny Hill than Casanova, surely? But she didn't trust him? This was news.

'You've seen what he's like. He says it's a laugh, that I'm no fun. He tells me he likes to keep the ladies happy, that's why he does it. He makes out the women know he's married, but they like to be flattered. He tells me it's good for business – just banter,' she pauses for breath, 'but he's a sex maniac, Maureen.'

I am blushing at this uncharacteristic disclosure. Uncharacteristic for my sister, for our family, for this time and this town. We don't talk like this here. Shirley looks round towards the ward door.

'He's coming in to see you after he's been to the wholesalers. It's half-day closing. You'll not say anything, will you? Well, you can't, can you. Sorry, that was tactless.'

Shirley gives one of her fake smiles to a nurse as she passes by and drops her voice again.

'I give him what he wants, *everything* he wants, but it doesn't stop him. He's always brushing past the women looking at the carpet samples, making sure there's a box in the way so he has to squeeze past. Each of them thinks they're the only one getting the attention. One New Year's Eve, I found him at one of the Christmas temps. They were in the store room and he was on his knees with his head up her skirt. I sent her home, locked the shop, wiped his face and lay over the counter so he could have what he wanted. That's when I started to take the money. I take it so we can't afford any staff. It's as simple as that.'

I try not to recreate the scene in my imagination. Shirley and George in the shop, on the counter. Her wiping his face. I wondered if she'd used her hand or a tissue. Then I wondered if he'd been wearing his navy shop overall with *McNair's* embroidered on the pocket.

I forced myself to focus on remembering the shop. George's side had Polyfilla, and rat poison and fire-guards, and the other – Shirley's – had Pyrex jugs and melamine trays decorated with pictures of grapes and cheese. The shop had originally been two shops and indeed, the two halves were still fairly separate with a doorway joining the two. That was where George had the best opportunity to get up close and personal with most of the local women. There was apparently never enough money to renovate and improve the shop so they continued to work in the cluttered space, climbing ladders to fetch plungers or paper plates while customers waited in the queue.

Every morning, George wheeled out a range of outdoor goods to sit displayed under the orange awning on the wide pavement in front of the shop: picnic chairs and barbecues and gardening tools. I used to wonder why Shirley went to work in the shop when she could have been a legal secretary. I suppose she did it to keep an eye on her man – the playboy of Derryconnor. But George would always try to get round it. When she was indoors in fancy goods he would exit by the door on his side and stand among the rakes eyeing up the passing housewives.

In comes George now, all swagger and smiles as if he is walking onto a chat show.

'Well, Maureen,' he says jauntily, 'I've always wanted to get you in bed.'

Shirley looks at me with a 'see what I mean' face. She has moved onto the end of my bed so that George can sit on the plastic hospital chair.

'A couple of sisters too. Every man's dream.'

'Away on with you, George,' says Shirley.

'Only kidding, my love,' he grins, grabbing Shirley's hand.

Then: 'No, seriously, Maureen darling, Are you all right? The old talking's not good, I hear. Never worry, you never get a word in edgeways with me anyway.'

He and Shirley talk across me for half an hour, occasionally bringing me in with an 'isn't that right Maureen?' George's eyes stray towards the nurses' station.

'Uniforms aren't what they used to be,' he says. 'No stockings these days.'

'Would you hold your whist, George?' Shirley cuts in. 'Maureen doesn't want to hear your chat. It's not decent.'

He leans over and whispers something in her ear. She shakes her head but she's smiling at him. They have something. It is weird and dysfunctional, but they have something.

When George left to drop the goods off at the shop, Shirley stayed behind. I thought she would be embarrassed at what she had revealed earlier but she continues as if there had been no interruption.

'You see why I couldn't have any girls in the shop. He knows he has never had a chance with you. It's still... humiliating for me.' She articulates the word as if she had only thought it in the past and never before felt it form in her mouth. 'Even if I know I can trust you. When he goes on like that, it can make me cross. All that hugging and sliding his hand towards your arse. I think that's why Claire doesn't come home. She hates that side of him – not that he'd ever do anything to her... No, don't ever worry about that. Anyway, I'll head home. He'll want his tea.'

Shirley was smiling as she left.

Would Billy have been like that? Billy was a charmer; much, much better at it than George.

11

Last night I dreamed of kisses. Whose kisses? I do not know. It was dark in the dream but if I had opened my eyes I could have seen who was kissing me. He was taller than me. I had to tip-toe up; he had to bend down. In the dream I could control time and so I could replay it again and again. At the beginning of the sequence he was standing in front of me holding both my hands. Then he moved one hand to my shoulder and one to the back of my head, gently tilting my face to meet his mouth. That moment before the kiss – the 'is he? isn't he?' moment – lasted for a long time and it was that sequence I replayed most.

*

Walter didn't like kissing. I asked him about it once, soon after we married.

'Do you not like kissing me?' I said. I tried not to sound hurt.

'I'm not one for kissing,' he said.

'I like kissing. It's important for me.' I couldn't bear the thought of that being it.

'Not for me.' Conversation over.

I was furious. The fury manifested itself audibly in a sort of growl. Walter left the room and I began to whimper. No more kisses for Mrs McCormack.

So, last night I dreamed of kisses and I didn't know who was kissing me but I knew it wasn't him. And now I'm thinking of all the kisses I ever had or rather, all those moments just before a potential kiss. Kiss chase, boys being dared to kiss, boys walking me to the bus stop, young men parking their smoky

Cortinas at the end of the lane when they were dropping me home, men who needed encouragement, men who needed no encouragement. And then Walter, whose kisses gradually faded and dried like a letter left in the sun.

Anyway, not enough kisses. I don't think I've had my quota. So is it any wonder that each time I saw Tom Kelso, I imagined things. Each time he came for the spring water, I imagined those moments before a kiss.

*

For a long time we've bottled the spring water. There's a pipe that brings the water from the old spring house to a new out-house, all white tiles and health and safety now. You have to run the sterilising fluid through the taps before you fill the bottles and then seal and label. It's cold work. I sell to the local hotels. Could I quote Father Toolis on the label, saying, 'It's so pure it doesn't need to be blessed'? Or Marjorie Mckillop, the midwife, who used to talk about the 'Stavey Spring babies', as she's so sure of the power of the water to increase fertility – though of course that talk all stopped when Jackie was born.

The doctor still came for the water. Year after year; the perfect twin boys in hand-knitted and later expensive bought jerseys sat in the car. They were pleasant enough. They would wave to Jackie and say, 'Hello, Mrs McCormack,' or 'Thanks, Mrs Mc-Cormack,' if I brought them out a biscuit. Why did he keep coming, like a cousin calling on relations? I couldn't work out if I was kidding myself that he wanted me. I felt those hands on me. I felt that heart beating as I leaned my head against him. It was a kind of madness.

One day he called for water on the way back from dropping the boys somewhere. I tried to keep him, with chat about the roadworks or plans for the new Health Centre. Anything, really.

'I'd better get off home now,' he said. 'I'm off today. Elizabeth will be looking for me to cut the grass.'

He looked tired and resentful or did I just want to believe that? I imagined her standing in the garden looking at her watch. She'd be wearing something impractical like white trousers and probably be carrying a basket of newly snipped roses. Elizabeth. You could never imagine anyone shortening it. She would never be a Liz and certainly not a Lizzie. She'd already have done her make-up, her thin wide lips looking as if they'd been stamped on, her hair controlled and sprayed. She'd never forget to wear gardening gloves.

I see them at church every Sunday, him stiffly holding her arm like an uncomfortable father of the bride as they walk to their pew. She has a rotation of half a dozen perfect little suits which she wears with exactly the right amount of jewellery and elegant shiny shoes. She often smiles as she passes, like a mayoress on walkabout. Does she have any idea, I wonder, of the secret plans I have had for her husband? A day off together and she wants him to garden. If he were mine I wouldn't stand around pruning while he marched behind a diesel lawnmower. We would kiss in a wild garden while the untended rose petals tumbled around us.

*

My sister has obviously read somewhere that it's good to talk to people in hospital even if they can't respond. She has talked more to me in the past few days than in the last twenty years. It is visiting time again and she walks in, sits by my bed and launches straight in as if she is continuing a conversation.

'You changed, Maureen, after you went away that time. Did you have an abortion? They would tell me nothing but I knew something had changed in you. You stopped looking at me and

83

you walked differently, as if you were ashamed. Mother told me I must ask you nothing, that you'd been sick and you weren't to be reminded of it. She said you'd been staying with Auntie Helen in England. At first I thought you were dying, of TB – it was the only illness I knew about. Then I knew it was because of that boy, the one who went back to America. But it was more than a love sickness. More than love sickness for any man, anyway.'

And maybe I'll tell her some day. For a while now it's been a secret I no longer have to keep. I can choose to share it now. I have no one to anger or protect. My parents can no longer be shamed and my husband cannot feel deceived. I know I can trust Shirley and always could really. But keeping secrets is a habit which is hard to break. She wants the best for me but she is being startlingly frank now and our barrier to communication seems to be gone. She is pulling bobbles off her acrylic jersey and starts again.

'Walter used to talk to me sometimes, you know. He'd come into the shop after the mart. "You're stinking," I'd say. "Get out of my nice clean shop," but he knew I was codding. I used to think he and I would have been better suited than...' she nodded towards me. 'But I just *thought* it. Nothing happened. It was only daydreaming when George had been drinking and acting the fool. Walter seemed more of a man, someone I could respect.'

Shirley is still picking at the jersey to avoid meeting my eye. 'You didn't love him, did you? He knew that. To be honest, I felt you were cruel to marry him. I shouldn't be saying that now, not with you... and with him long gone. It's all too late.

'He would tell me that you never looked at him. He thought it was like one of those arranged marriages that the Indians have. He was a farmer without a farm and you were going to get a farm and had no farmer. It suited everybody but you... and him. He blamed the doctor, you know. Walter said you had had your head turned by Tom Kelso. And he didn't even know what I knew. That night of Claire's engagement party... We never even talked about the engagement party either,' said Shirley. 'Never talked about what happened and we were sisters. What sort of sisters... ?'

'Yes,' I say. I try to say sorry but it comes out sounding like 'Sunday'.

Although Shirley normally keeps on talking, she trails off because even with her newfound frankness, she can't face this. I close my eyes and think about the engagement party.

Claire had got engaged to one of the Kelso boys – I can't even remember which one now. Elizabeth Kelso was furious. Claire was an eccentric even in those days. Just out of drama school. She bought second-hand clothes from junk shops. All petticoats showing, odd buttons and woolly tights. The boy was going to be a vet. Elizabeth Kelso was spitting mad but the Kelso boy was crazy about Claire. That night she looked lovely. Even Elizabeth Kelso said so. She walked into the room in a silk dress and you could have believed she was on the way to collect an Oscar. When the Kelso boy kissed her, she lifted one foot off the ground like in the films. I was never quite sure whether it was accidental or for effect. She looked like a 1930s starlet.

Claire enjoyed the idea of a wedding day – she joked that she couldn't wait to get rid of the name Claire McNair – but I'm not sure she seriously thought she would be married. I'm upset even thinking about that evening. There was too much drink around. We are not drinking people, us Ulster Protestants. We're not as bad as Paisley's lot, we'll have a glass or two at a celebration, but I wasn't used to it. There was champagne. Actual real champagne. Elizabeth Kelso wanted to do it properly, even if the girl wasn't right. She had flowers sent from Belfast.

Jackie was there and had got very tired. Walter had offered to take her home. He wasn't one for parties anyway. There were a lot of young ones around. They were dancing and loud. Elizabeth Kelso was shooing them away from the door if they were smoking. Gracious shooing, but that's what it was.

My sister's in a talking mood again.

'I know that it annoyed you, when Claire did things. The engagement highlighted it again. You knew Jackie would never have that. It made you feel bad.'

And she was right, in a way. I loved Claire. I loved her so much, but everything she did that Jackie couldn't was hard for me.

I felt very sorry for myself that night of the engagement party. I should have gone with Walter and Jackie. I said that I'd stay to help Elizabeth clear up, but that's not why I stayed. I wanted to be part of his world for a while. It was only about the third or fourth time I had been to the house, and mostly it had been to charity things. A garden party for Sierra Leone, a coffee morning for deaf children – that sort of thing. I was foolish. Still am.

'I never gossiped,' my sister continues, 'never told anyone else. His name would have been mud, if people had known.'

Walter had phoned the Kelsos from our house and asked me to find Jackie's blanket. It had been renamed 'the shawl' but it was really a security blanket. She wrapped it round her in times of stress. Tom Kelso walked past me in the hall as I took the call. I was thinking how it was odd to have a phone in a hall, but it was from the days when the phone was functional – used only for emergencies.

'Is everything okay?' Tom asked.

'The shawl is missing.' He knew about the shawl. 'I've been told I can't come home without it.'

'Shall I organise a search?'

'I think we might need to organise a posse from Ballinstavey barracks.'

'I'll give you a hand.' We looked downstairs, moving drunk

twenty-one year olds to check under cushions and chairs. Shirley was still all 'mother-of-the-bride' with a new dress and her answering machine voice, trying to talk to people. She was stone cold sober because she was driving and preferred it that way anyway so she could keep an eye on George, drunk as a lord and flirting with girls in their teens, wobbling on high heels on Elizabeth's Persian rugs.

Jackie had been everywhere in the house. I'd found her in the guest bathroom experimenting with the liquid soap earlier.

'I'm going to have a look round upstairs. If that's okay? I'm afraid Jackie's done a tour of the whole house. It could be any-where.'

Tom Kelso walked up the stairs beside me. It was all in my imagination but I had got to the stage where even walking up the stairs seemed wrong and risky. As if we would be in trouble if anyone saw us.

'I've spent half my life searching for this,' I said, mock wearily.

As we turned at the top of the stair he put his hand in the small of my back.

'So have I, Maureen.' It was his voice as much as what he said that made me blush. An instant school girl blush that other women would assume was a symptom of 'the change' but it wasn't the lack of hormones that was the problem here. He opened a door and steered me as he had when we danced. He stood right behind me. I looked around the room for the missing blanket as if I had a walk-on part in an am-dram farce. I'd have been picked out for over-acting even by the *Chronicle*. His hands were on my shoulders and his mouth on my neck. We were on the bed in seconds.

Eighteen years. Eighteen years of looks across the pews at church, of holding my hand when I was upset about Jackie, of standing too close for photographs at church events and a con-gratulatory kiss or two after a charity badminton match.

Eighteen years of moments leading to this. Leading to me with my new dress around my waist and Tom inside me, saying how much he wanted me, loved me... I was holding him close. His hands were in my hair and I felt fierce and angry with love for him.

I had heard Shirley shouting up the stairs but I didn't care. There were footsteps.

'I've found it!' she shouted as she walked into the room holding 'the shawl' towards me. 'It was on the back of the cloak-room door.' She stood there. I just wanted her to go. I didn't feel embarrassed or regretful. I felt cross that she didn't just leave.

'It's not what you think. Get out!' I cried at her that night in the spare bedroom at the Kelsos'. She knew – would have known even had she not walked into the guest room that night or not seen my scrubbed face and the rumpled dress as I slipped out through the side door later. It did change me.

He came round the next morning to see if I was okay. He said he had behaved badly and he hoped that it would cause no trouble for me. I took my cues from him. I had slept little that night and my fantasy was that he would come round and beg me to go away with him. When his car arrived in the yard, I was sure that's what was going to happen.

'It was the drink. Bad stuff. Devil's buttermilk – maybe Paisley has that right?'

I smiled.

'And the dancing,' he went on. 'It leads to all sorts of... Are you really all right? I am so, so sorry.'

He was saying sorry. Apologizing as if he had assaulted me. In my head it was so different.

'It was what I wanted.' I spoke quietly, looking down. 'It's what I want.'

'This cannot be, Maureen. We both know it. It cannot be.' He handed me a brown A5 envelope, unsealed. 'Read it carefully and decide. Telephone if you need me to explain anything.' He got in the car and I watched him drive off.

In the envelope were an early version of what they now call 'morning after pills' with a handwritten explanation of how to take them and a printed leaflet about side-effects. Another car in the yard. I still hadn't even brushed my hair. It was Shirley. I stuffed the information and the tablets back in the envelope.

'Nothing happened.'

'I saw his car.'

'Just don't start. Nothing happened.'

'I don't know how...'

'No. You *don't* know. So don't start.'

'I know it was the drink too. Far too much of it. George is lying at home this morning, moaning and boking into a bucket. Between the two of you, I...'

'Give over, Shirley.'

I wouldn't let her talk. I can see now that I did that to a lot of people. I stopped them and then complained that they didn't talk to me. I assumed I knew what they were going to say so I shut them up. But now I can't. I have to listen to my sister.

'When I walked in that night, I didn't know where to put myself. I was mesmerised. I couldn't think. I didn't know how long it had been going on for. I had seen you were miserable earlier that night. You were happy for Claire but in your eyes I could see sadness. You envied me for having a daughter that was normal. You envied Elizabeth for having Tom. You envied the young their youth. All your life you've focused on what you did not have, not what you did. Well, except Jackie. I'm not saying you didn't focus on Jackie.'

I am shocked that she would say such a thing. Not shocked at the content, for I recognise it as the truth, although no one – neither I nor anyone else – has ever confronted me with it. I am shocked that Shirley has seen it and known it and kept quiet all these years. How would I sum up my feelings about my life so far? 'It's not fair' or 'I could have been…' Not even a 'has been', a 'could have been' who wasn't and blamed everybody else.

I begin to cry, with grief and still some shame. Shirley fusses with tissues and tuts and 'there theres'.

'I know I shouldn't be hard on you but it has been hard for me too. Hard not to show I am proud of Claire or happy about good things when they happen. Hard seeing my sister take no pleasure from anything and waste her whole bloody life.'

I have never heard Shirley swear. She knew it would make me listen.

'If you wanted to have an affair, you should have just done it or left Walter. I knew what you felt about Tom. Anybody with any gumption could tell. Why have all the gossip and guilt of it all – and do nothing? You needed to make things happen instead of waiting and blaming and envying.'

Could I have taken Tom Kelso in my arms and said, 'Come with me. This can be – we both want it'? Could I have had an affair and got it out of my system one way or the other? That morning I let him hand me that envelope. It could have had plane tickets in it, but it didn't. I sat around waiting for people to hand me solutions in brown envelopes.

12

'You're lucky to be tucked up in here,' says Sister, who came on duty at lunchtime. She says it as if she really means it, as if she wishes she'd had a stroke and had landed up in hospital. 'It would blow you away out there – real kite-flying weather.' She pats her hair as though checking for lasting wind damage.

I love kites. Jackie and I would go up to the high field at any opportunity. It would keep her happy for hours. It was something she could do as well as anyone else, since it was so random whether the wind picked the kite up or dashed it down. We exhausted ourselves taking it in turns to be either the 'holder' as Jackie called it or the 'lifter', flinging the kite into the air. Then I'd look at my watch and realise two hours had gone by and we'd have to gather everything up and run back down the lane to the house to start cooking.

'I don't see the point of kites,' Walter would say.

'That's the whole idea of them,' I'd tell him. 'There *is* no point. It's completely for fun. You can't think of anything else while you are doing it.' Claire would sometimes come along but she would be looking for a system, for patterns in the wind, whereas Jackie let the elements take control. Looking upwards, birling round and round until she fell. When both girls were there, there was no need for me to be on holding or lifting duty and I would sit on a low branch of a tree, always wishing I'd brought a book or a flask or an extra jumper. It didn't suit me to have too much time to think, never has. Yet that's all I can do now. If I wasn't caught up in the running and chasing of kite-flying I was thinking of what else I could have been doing... what life might have brought me. Always struggling against the here and now and never seeing how much there was to cherish, like my darling girl, so warm and loving and funny.

There is no real need for me to be in bed but they tell me I need the rest.

'You don't realise it, but the physio really takes it out of you. Take the rest while you can, Mrs McCormack'.'

I am walking fairly well now. Everyone is 'very pleased with me' in a patronising way as if all I had to do is put a bit of effort in. It seems to be luck really. The Zimmer frame will be going soon, thank God. When I ditch that I'll get a stick eventually. Some day I'll be like the lads who lead the marching bands on the Twelfth of July. I'll twirl my stick and throw it up in the air, catching it without missing a beat, walking in time to 'The Sash' or 'Derry's Walls'. I hate the sentiment of the Orange men and the whole Protestant marching band ritual but it's hard not to fall for the boy at the front of the band with his swagger and con-tortions as he reaches to catch the stick behind him.

In the end I do fall asleep and the nurses come to help me up before visiting. I can nearly manage myself but the nice little student nurse called Tanya watches over me; screens are pulled round to protect my dignity as I flounder about. When I am as pre-sentable as I can be, having ditched the horrible yellow dressing gown that Shirley selected for me at the Dunne's stores sale, Tanya pulls the curtain back. At the door I can see Shirley's George, hov-ering and giving a half-wave. Tanya beckons him over.

'She's all yours,' says Tanya.

'Oh, if only she was, eh Maureen?' George is consistent; I'll say that for him.

'Yes,' I say in a weary way.

'You're still no more chat, then? Never mind, I like a girl who can't say no.' He starts to sing a song he half-remembers. ''I'm just a girl who can't say no...' and then he peters out. 'Sorry, Maureen, only kidding, – you know me.'

George pauses as if centring himself.

'Shirley's over at the Centre picking up Jackie. They had some sort of trip out today. I said I'd drop by, the shop being shut and all. So are they treating you all right here?' He looks round the ward, then back at me. 'She'll swing past later with Jacks.' He fidgets for a while then, as if unable to cope with a silent audience. 'But at least you have me now.'

He points and flexes his foot in a way that looks almost feminine even though he is wearing heavy boots. He looks nervous, as if waiting for something. 'It's not the same without Walter, is it? And now you in here. Shirley and me, we're better with company. Claire livens the place up for a wee while but then she's off again. Then the pressure's on me again. You know your sister. Always giving off about something. She likes to be in control, so she does. It doesn't suit me.'

George leans over and picks up yesterday's *Belfast Telegraph* from the table and goes quiet again. George was good-looking in his day and now his looks have let him down and he is uneasy about it. He is still squeezing himself into the same jeans he wore in his badminton-playing days and he has developed a habit of plucking at his polo shirt when he sits down, to make sure it doesn't cling to his spare tyre. There is a mark along the side of his head where his driving glasses have made an indent. His light brown hair has virtually no grey, making me suspect he touches it up a bit. It has developed a fluffiness on the top that suggests it's not going to stay for long. He turns the pages in the paper as if an actor on stage, waiting for his cue. George's hands are soft and hairless. Despite him selling hardware and gardening products, Shirley does all the work at home. George is always off at a Masonic meeting or there is something on at the Orange Hall. Meanwhile Shirley slogs on single-handed.

'When are you getting rid of this yoke?' He points to the walking frame which they have tucked round the back of my chair, but he doesn't wait for an answer. 'To be honest, Maureen, she's driving me mad. I need to get off on my own sometimes... to sort things out. But she'll have none of it. "I've got plenty for you to sort out here," she'll say, and then she hands me some list. I'm scunnered looking at her lists. A man needs a bit of free time. Like next week, I have to take somebody to the airport. I shouldn't need to explain the whole thing to Shirley, should I? There's somebody that needs to get to Manchester for an appointment that she – that *they* need to keep private. So how would I get down to Aldergrove without Shirley knowing? But I owe it to this person. And they need picking up the next day.'

George sits sighing and fiddling with his mobile phone. 'I can't even trust her not to check my phone, for God's sake. Paranoid she is, your sister.' Then: 'What am I going to do? She's only nineteen, this girl. What am I going to do?'

George looks me in the eye. He knows I know what this is about. He sniffs and scratches and shifts in his chair. 'Only nineteen and she's interested in me.' A quick smile. George can't help boasting despite the angst.

Some wee girl having to go off on her own to get an abortion. What a bastard, I think. A prat, a lech, a shit, a real shit. And he's telling me to make himself feel better. I try to tell him to fuck off but it sounds like 'fluff'. I ring the bell. The Sister comes, smiling,

'She's doing very well. We're very pleased with her.'

'But the speech – it's completely gone. There's no chance of getting that back, is there?' George's look is not one of solicitude.

'She's still getting the speech therapy. You never know. Slow but sure.' She turns to me. 'Is that old head bothering you again, love?'

I do have a headache now, but pressing the button was about getting rid of George. Sister goes to get me a paracetamol.

'I shouldn't have worried you, Maur'. Don't worry. Everything'll be hunky dory.' George lowers his voice. 'It was a one-off thing. She was all over me. I gave in – it was a one-off.' He gives me a serious – or is it a warning look? 'Shirley should not know. You know I love her. That's why I have to get round the airport problem... And here they are, the lovely ladies.' George reverts to his old blustery way of talking.

Shirley and Jackie are laden with stuff and George immediately slips off – to deal with his dilemma, no doubt.

'I had a flask.' There is no preamble with Jackie. 'It didn't break.'

'I only said it could easily break,' says Shirley.

'She hid it.'

'I did not hide it.' Shirley laughs, but I believe Jackie. 'Let's forget about that and tell your mum about the trip.'

'I had tea,' says Jackie, pausing for effect. 'We saw goats. You can't take your packed lunch near the goats.'

'And there was a baby goat, wasn't there?' Shirley means well and she looks pleased that Jackie has enjoyed the day. 'Tell her about the baby goat, Jackie.'

'It was new. Anyway it's a kid, not a baby goat. But you can't hold it.'

'Joan from the Centre took some pictures. Will you bring the pictures in to show Mum when she gets them printed?'

'I'll bring them in when she gets them printed. I'll give you a hug.' She gives me a classic Jackie hug with a loud kiss. 'Is your leg better?'

Shirley answers for me.

'It's not completely right yet, Jackie. But they say they're very pleased with you, Maureen.'

I nod and smile. Shirley looks tired. Jackie *is* tiring. George is always trying to escape from any responsibility so I expect she's doing everything on her own. How could George still be getting himself into these ridiculous situations at his age?

Jackie takes some hand-cream out of my locker before Shirley can stop her. She sticks a finger into the jar and dots it over my affected hand. Then she rubs it in carefully, taking her time, showing patience I have not seen in her before. The cream is supposed to smell of honey and roses but somehow it smells of fresh air and freedom. I thought of all the times I had held her hand or rubbed her back when she was a wee colicky baby. I nearly cry with love for her but I hold it in because I know it will upset her. Jackie reaches for the cream again and Shirley tries to halt her.

'I'm sure that's enough cream.'

'The other hand isn't done.'

'Yes, yes, yes,' I say, holding the other hand up and thinking, It's my fucking hand cream. I am starting to feel angry more often. I suppose that might be a good sign. Perhaps I wasn't even well enough to feel cross before.

'Okay, but don't go mad with it,' says Shirley.

I shake my head and so does Jackie as she takes a generous handful of cream and covers me almost to the elbow. Shirley pointedly puts a towel under my arm to gain some dignity in this mini-defeat. She starts to tell me what she's been doing.

'There was a fair few at the fork supper last night. Jackie came too. You were very good, weren't you?'

'I was good,' said Jackie. Although I don't think she's capable of it, I imagine I hear sarcasm in Jackie's absent-minded comment as she works on my hands.

'Jackie had a big chat with the Kelsos. Didn't you, darlin'? They were asking for you. Elizabeth Kelso co-ordinated the whole thing. And the Reverend Purdie was saying he'd come in to see you. I wasn't sure if you would be mad about that idea – but it's the thought that counts, isn't it. George couldn't come last night. He has some meeting or something. I don't know who with, for most of his cronies were there last night. But you know what he's like. They seek him here, they seek him there, that dammed elusive George McNair. I have to do the flowers at church this week – your turn. I don't see why I should inherit my sister's place on the flower rota. Oh well. I'll do my best.'

Jackie continues to rub my hand and Shirley tells me every single thing on the menu last night. Everyone had brought a dish to share and Shirley passes judgement on everyone's efforts this morning. Someone had the cheek to bring bought meringues.

'They were so bland! Honestly, when you think of the lovely meringues our mother used to make. People don't seem to care any more.'

'I'm hungry,' says Jackie.

I'm fed up with the talk about desserts and start to get up, pointing towards the bathroom. Jackie walks with me, really close, her hands out to catch as if she is marking me in a netball match. I let go of the walking frame and show that I am really steady now but she doesn't want to take a chance. I did not think she would be capable of this much care. She has learned a lot over the past few weeks. She counts as I walk.

'One, two, three, four, five. One two three four...' She starts again and then we both say *five*. Jackie is laughing, saying, 'One, two, three, four, five, once I caught a fish alive.' I find I can join in and Jackie claps. She waits outside the loo door, singing to me, the way I used to sing to her to reassure her I was still there.

Jackie has made me another card. *I love you* she has written, surrounded by hearts – one member of the family that has no problem expressing emotions. My mother and father couldn't have said it and felt uncomfortable when I was affectionate to Jackie or Claire.

'You'll spoil those weans with all that kissing and hugging.'

Jackie and I have a hug and rub noses and walk back to my bed.

When we get back, Tom Kelso is there.

'We were talking about the Soroptimist fork supper,' Shirley is saying. 'Do you know how much they raised, Tom?'

'Elizabeth had me counting the ticket money at midnight. We think seven hundred.'

'That's great. Elizabeth's a natural party organiser, I don't know what we'd do without her. Tom's here visiting someone, Maureen. I caught him on the way through.' She nods towards me. 'They're very pleased with her.'

Again I take my hands off the frame and flourish a wave.

'Great news. You're looking a lot better.'

Claire has been out to the shops for me. I am wearing a new navy tracksuit instead of the floral nighties. I look incongruously sporty but just the wearing of it makes me feel fitter.

Shirley was back to the food conversation. Coronation chicken, a quiche with sardines in it, a very nice rice salad, but with walnuts, which she didn't like.

'I'm hungry,' says Jackie. 'Are there any biscuits?' She looked around hopefully.

'It's nearly teatime. Just hold on, Jackie.'

'I'm rumbling.' Jackie is revving up to make a fuss.

'Okay, we'll get on. Nice to see you, Tom.' Shirley looks at Tom Kelso as if she expects him to leave first. There is a moment's silence then she continues, 'Well, we'll go. Say hello to Elizabeth for us.' As she walks out of the ward, she glances back, looking disapproving as he sits down on the chair she has left.

'Are you okay? She never stops, does she? I think it's nerves. We were sitting beside her at the do last night. I managed to swap so I could talk to Jackie. A better conversationalist any day – and she knows about taking turns. I liked talking to Jackie. It made me feel closer to you. Jackie has been our chaperone really all those years. I could never have spent all that time with you without her there, could I?'

He picks up a card from the locker by my bed. It's the one from my art evening class.

'Elizabeth hasn't been in, has she?'

'Yes.'

'She's been in?' Tom looks surprised. 'She never mentioned it.'

And he never mentions to her that he's been in. I can tell he's unsettled by the thought of us being alone together. I am curious about what he thinks would happen.

He leans towards me and we both smile at the same time.

'You smell nice, what is it?'

I lift the tub of hand cream to show him and point it towards my hand. He lifts the weaker hand up and examines it. He straightens the fingers and strokes each finger gently. 'Very soft. Probably the longest rest they've ever had.' He glances around. There have not been many visitors today as it is midweek. He lifts my hand up and kisses the inside of my wrist.

He smiles his risky smile and leans a bit closer, keeping eye-contact.

'Elizabeth and her parties. I think a lot about that night. That party at our house.' He looks downward. I can feel myself blushing. 'Bloody hell, Maureen, I don't know what came over me. I felt out of control. I had to have you. I think I was rough. I worried I was rough. But you were... I knew you were...' His voice slows and steadies and he looks me in the eye again. 'You were keen too, I think.'

It wasn't a question but I nod my head slowly.

'Then I lost my nerve. I knew it couldn't be undone but also knew that it was easier if it wasn't acknowledged with words. As it was, we could both blame the champagne, but if we had actually had to name what had happened, what we were really feeling, there would be no going back. So the morning after, I thought I could "draw a line under it" as they say – for both of us. I was a coward. I wasn't ready to handle the fall-out: telling

Elizabeth, the disruption to Jackie, Walter... The farm was your family farm. You and Walter couldn't split up. It was both your home and his livelihood. I would have to leave the practice – even risk getting struck off, as you were still registered with me. I didn't have the strength to go through with it, but nor did I have the restraint to stop myself that night. But the fact that I drew that line was not an indication of the strength of my feelings for you – you do understand that, don't you?'

Before he came round that morning after the engagement party, I tried to get down to some housework, distracted by the dry, fluttery agitation of a champagne hangover and a feeling of promise. Then his arrival, the brown envelope of pills – and sitting alone on the side of the bath, slurping from the wash-basin tap, swallowing pill after pill, as if I were taking an overdose. After his visit, the hangover had changed to thudding pressure combined with sorrow and shame. It brought back the same shame I had felt all those years before when I sat in the nursing home on the outskirts of Glasgow, tired from the ferry train from Stranraer and the heaviness of a pregnancy I couldn't celebrate.

Still I forgave him, if not myself. I had been a grown woman of forty-two. That night I had weighed it all up, perhaps not waited for the scales to balance, but I made a decision to go ahead. He did not know how sad I had been, how much had been invested in that evening, unplanned but yet planned for years.

And what do I feel as he sits before me now? I don't know. I am nobody's wife now, but if there were good reasons for not going for it then, there are different but equal ones today. Even if I do emerge from this hospital unscathed, I'll have a medical history that no one should lightly take on. Jackie is still dependent on me, and Elizabeth, older now, has even more invested in their life together.

Soon, none of us will care about passion and sex, even George. When it comes down to it, one day what is going to be important is someone to hold our hand while we lie dying. Does Elizabeth deserve that more than me, for I have other hands to hold?

13

Shirley and I always had projects. Rarely was there spontaneous play. Our games were ongoing and had names. Even at the beach, if we built a sandcastle we would not be content to let it be washed away. Shirley would insist on robust defences: stone reinforced walls. She thought we could stop the tide if only we worked hard enough. Although I was the elder, she would often be in charge.

One project I remember went on for months: wall cleaning. Now I realise how long it takes lichen to grow but Shirley saw it as nature's graffiti and was determined to eradicate it from our property. Every day one summer, we sat in the shade of the garden wall scraping with our nails or bits of slate.

'We have to get on with our work,' she would say, when I begged to dress dolls or rest in the sun. So we'd continue scraping, in silence, knuckles white with tension, occasionally stopping to admire our progress. If I ever get home again I'll look at that wall to see if nature is winning again. The house where I live now is the house I grew up in. I've lived on the farm for most of my life apart from the short stint in Glasgow in the home for unwed mothers and my time at teacher-training college. Walter and I lived in a small cold bungalow down the hill from the house just after we got married. When Jackie was expected we moved back in with Mother so that she could help. The idea was that she and my father would move to the bungalow and Dad would retire.

*

The nice nurse called Tanya likes me. That's not why she's nice to me. I think she's nice to everyone but she does seem to like talking to me. Today she asked if she could use me as a case study for her essay.

'Yes.'

'I only asked you because I know you'll say yes,' she says. She laughs mischievously and I raise a fist at her in jest.

'No seriously, it's all confidential, but I would like your agreement.'

I nod and smile and wish I could help her more. It was cold yesterday and Tanya kept her cardigan on in the morning, which is against the rules. When the Ward Sister came in unexpectedly, she hid it in my locker along with the mystery man's scarf, so now I feel we are allies. She's not that much older than I was when I got pregnant that first time, but she seems so much more mature and thoughtful. Worldly-wise but not in a bad way. In control. She's got a boyfriend, she tells me as she sorts out the bed.

'But it's not serious yet,' she says.

I wonder what that means nowadays. Does it mean that they haven't had sex or maybe that they haven't met each other's parents. It's all different nowadays. Girls look after themselves. Back when I got pregnant at eighteen, I was buffeted about on my mother and father's choices for me. Everything was left undiscussed, even when it should have been too late for embarrassment.

My father drove me to the ferry in virtual silence. I wondered if he had been told not to speak to me or, more likely, whether he did not know what to say. He had been treating me very gently since the news emerged. This was in contrast to my mother, who had encouraged me to keep busy and had me climbing ladders and carrying heavy buckets as if playing fast and loose with my pregnancy. It was in the days before wheelie suitcases and my father stopped at a shop in Larne to buy some wheels for my luggage. In the car park of the ferry terminal, he strapped the big mock leather case to the trolley. When he waved me goodbye, I could see he feared he was saying farewell to a daughter as well as a grandchild.

I was on the deck of the ferry for most of the crossing. Pregnancy seemed to have lowered the threshold for sea sickness and I couldn't bear the greasy thick air of the passenger lounge. The seagulls swooped and shrieked around me like pterodactyls. Despite my growing bump I felt I was so insubstantial that they could have lifted me and flown away with me. As we approached port at Stranraer, I returned to my suitcase and the family I had asked to mind it for me.

'Will you be able to manage this big case?' said the woman, nodding towards my middle. Despite the long scarf arranged to drape over my front, she knew. She was the only person outside my family who had seen, and the first person to look at me with sympathy.

'I'm okay. The sickness will stop as soon as we get landed.' I neither confirmed nor denied anything. The skirt my mother had adapted to accommodate my shape was cutting into me and my coat seemed tight even across my shoulders. I felt that soon I might burst out of my clothes like an un-pricked sausage under a grill.

On the train, my suitcase was lifted onto the luggage rack by a young soldier without me even asking. Everyone seemed to be smoking but I couldn't be bothered to see if there was a non-smoking compartment. I kept my leather gloves on for the whole journey because I couldn't bear anyone to see that I wasn't married. I was tired but scared to sleep. I had a big envelope of cash in my handbag for the Home and a smaller one with some notes to pay the taxi. I sat by the window, cheek resting against smeary glass watching it rain on Barrhill, Girvan, Maybole and

Ayr, and then hail on Prestwick. I dozed with my handbag straps wound tight around my fingers, waking up at Kilwinning station. From there to Glasgow I became increasingly anxious about the details of negotiating the taxi rank. I had never got a taxi on my own before.

My mother had told me several times to make sure I got a price before I got in the cab but I just said, 'Here, please,' as I handed the piece of paper with the address to the taxi driver. He was friendly as he carried my bag to the door of the big solid house, but I imagined he looked disappointed in me.

I shared a room in the home with a very young, frightened girl from near Aberdeen. Her due date was her fifteenth birthday. Disclosure of any information was discouraged and the staff asked nothing. Everyone acted as if we had inconveniently been the victims of Immaculate Conception. There are horror stories about such mother and baby homes, but the staff at this place were kind. The Green Grove Home for Unwed Mothers was a Presbyterian concern. The staff were unnecessarily aproned and starched during work hours but I suspect didn't loosen up much at home. We watched them walking down the drive at the end of their work day, in their Harris Tweed skirts and Christian shoes. This was missionary work for them and they were driven. They knitted continually during their breaks – bonnets and bootees for our little bastards. They were good women.

We were strictly regimented at the Home. After breakfast we had a walk in the garden. There were about a dozen of us at any one time deemed fit for walking and we did circuit after circuit of this medium- sized garden, like prisoners in an exercise yard. We were led mostly by Miss McKenzie, an older lady with sunspots on her face, who would talk about her time in Rhodesia. The walks were good-natured and sometimes playful. We would fall into step with whoever was leading and pretend to march, or all develop limps or funny walks. Miss McKenzie would stop and pretend to be annoyed before she launched into another story about her good work.

We were made to have afternoon rests but we would all sneak into one room, pull two beds together and recline, playing cards or the Truth Game. In the Truth Game, we took it in turns to tell stories about our lives, and the others had to say what was true and what was a lie. There were stories about us carrying babies of royal heritage, of being shipwrecked or living in castles. It was just storytelling, what women have done through the ages round cooking fires when they didn't have access to books.

Agnes had the best story-telling voice: 'I was born fifteen years and three days ago, the daughter of a Moroccan sailor called...' she paused for a moment '... a sailor called Arunuska Del Mar and a poor girl who worked in a fish factory in Fraserborough.'

'Aye, we believe the second bit.' There were always interruptions.

'Shh, let the lassie speak.'

'My father and mother met at the harbour. He had never seen red hair before. They fell in love and before my mother knew it, she was expecting me.'

'You left a bit out.' All the girls made kissing or whistling sounds but Agnes sighed and continued.

'Before my mother knew she was expecting me, my father left to sail the Seven Seas.'

'Are there only seven seas?'

'When he was leaving to sail the Seven Seas, she cut off six inches of her flaming red hair and tied each end of the plait with a green ribbon and gave it to him to carry next to his heart.'

'Ahh, that is so romantic.'

'But then he perished on the sea.'

'For those in peril on the sea,' someone started singing.

'Shh, it's sad; she's talking about her dad.'

And so the storytelling went on. There were no books of interest to us in the Green Grove. No 'Penny Dreadfuls' as my mother described anything cheap and racy, no magazines, just improving books or mission pamphlets or guides to Scottish Churches.

I found a book on birds called *In the Manse Garden* by 'A Minister's Wife'. She didn't even give her name. We used to read it aloud in a very prim voice but emphasise things like Great TIT and COCK Robin, and then giggle like the schoolgirls most of us were. The Green Grove Presbyterian ladies chided us for not resting but they were glad we were happy and taking such an interest in ornithology.

Before our confinement, as they still called it, we had housework to do and other tasks like nappy folding, needlework or measuring out portions of food that were taken round weekly to poor families. We didn't get to go on the visits but the earnest Presbyterian staff would tell us about the terrible state of the Glasgow tenements they visited, and talk about the men who had taken to drink and the women and children who slept with their shoes on, ready to run. These stories were meant to be a warning to us but they became more like episodes of a gripping radio play we enjoyed while folding and darning and weighing. There were times when I felt almost happy there, suspended between girlhood and the uncertain future.

Some girls were going to keep their babies but most were not. The decision seemed to be fixed by their parents before arrival, and we got the message that the Home did not understand or welcome any last-minute indecision. None of the staff at the Green Grove seemed to have had any experience of hormones and their effect. The girls were often in concealed turmoil, writing coded letters to their seducers begging for rescue and a life together. Agnes, my room mate, was told she could only go home with a baby if she revealed who the father was. Her family would then torture and kill him, she was sure. She got one letter from her butcher-boy boyfriend, a bloodstained fingerprint in one corner, a description of the weather in Balmedie but no acknowledgement of their shared trouble. She told me her heart was breaking.

I knew I would never contact Billy. He was no good. I didn't even feel I liked him any more. I hoped the baby would get his looks, but nothing else. Billy had charmed me, this big jokey fellow with his film star accent and fading tan. I loved the way he manoeuvred me around the dance hall.

I met Billy at a dance at the Majestic Hotel down on the coast. It was my friend Jill's sister's twenty-first birthday. Three girls were sharing the party. We had spent two weeks prior to the event learning to smoke until we looked Parisian. We traipsed a whole day round the city looking for something to wear. In the end, frustrated by the choice in our price range, I bought a length of dramatic crimson material and a Butterick paper pattern and my mother made my dress. As usual I started it, but Mother took over. She carefully undid my stitching, muttering that she could not let me out in darts like that. The truth is, she wanted to do it. Doing things for me was the only way she could show that she loved me. She fussed about leaving generous seams in case I put on weight. I only wore it once. I grew out of it, but not in the way my mother thought.

Shirley acted as my dresser on the evening of the party, handing me each item of clothing and jewellery with unusual reverence. We put a chiffon scarf over my face to protect the dress from the make-up – or was it to protect the make-up from the dress? My young face looked as artificial as a geisha's that night. I picked up my clutch bag and walked through the guard of honour of my parents and Shirley, refusing one last time to take my old school coat in case it got chilly.

The radio was playing in the car, filling the yard with sounds of 'Are You Lonesome Tonight?' The front passenger got out and pulled the seat forward to allow me in. I struggled onto Jill's knee for there were four of us squashed in the back. I had to keep my head bowed forward to stop it rubbing on the ceiling of the low-slung car so I rested my hands on the top of the front seats. It wasn't until I got settled and the car had started along the back roads that I registered the unknown young man who had got out to let me in. He turned and smiled, his face near mine.

'Cigarette?' An American. I could feel Jill pinching my side.

'Thanks.'

The American boy put it between my lips and reached for his lighter. The car swung round a corner and I ended up slipping over to one side. I sat up again, giggling.

'I'd better keep it for later,' I said. 'I need both hands free to hold on.'

'I'll give you a fresh one later.' He gently took the cigarette from my Parisian lips and put it between his own. He turned to light the cigarette and then spoke to Jill's brother. 'Drive carefully, Jeff, you've got some real precious cargo in the back.'

Jill poked me again.

He looked so healthy. Perfect teeth. A strange thing for a girl of that age to think, but it flitted into my mind – perhaps like my dad sizing up a pedigree bull. The music was loud. The two boys in the back were smoking too but we refused to open the windows lest the wind ruffle up our hairdos. I tried not to look at the American for the rest of the journey. When we arrived, there was a fuss over parking and we got dropped off right at the front door. The American boy took my hand to help me out of the back of the car and then he took Jill's and helped her. Part of me was relieved; perhaps he was just really polite. The other part of me was jealous: I couldn't bear anyone else to get him.

In the Majestic, we went straight to the ladies'. I reapplied my lipstick in case any had come off on the cigarette – the cigarette that had gone in his mouth, past those perfect teeth.

'Well?' I looked at Jill in the mirror.

'He's an American.'

'I know *that*.'

'He's called Billy. He's Malcolm's second cousin. He's going to university in England but he's here for the summer. All summer.'

We both went 'Ooohh' and jumped up and down, hugging each other the way girls do.

The ballooned and ribboned dance hall was almost deserted when we arrived. Three overly embellished birthday cakes competed on a draped table at one end. Everyone was crowded in the bar getting tipsy before the party even started. The birthday girls entered with their presents and their entourage. Jill and I were new to this world. We stood languidly smoking for something to do, tapping the ash off unnecessarily after every little puff. When the dance started, I wished we'd spent more time practising dancing rather than smoking. Everyone looked so confident. We decided to get a drink.

I was going to have a lime and soda which was the whole go then. My parents had warned me against having even one alcoholic drink. I had made a promise which I was intending to stick to.

'What will you have?' said Billy, sliding through the crowd and catching my hand.

'I'll have a gin, please.'

Jill asked for a shandy and Billy set off, waving a ten-shilling note towards the bar.

'Do you like gin?' Jill asked.

'I'll soon find out.'

'Your mum'll kill you.'

'It might be worth it,' I said, looking towards Billy's broad shoulders. I imagined him building a log cabin for us.

'Don't act too easy, Maureen. He's very proper... for an American,' said Jill.

'You only met him half an hour before me,' I said.

'Maureen, I'm only giving you advice. I'm not after him. I don't want you to let yourself down.'

I decided very quickly that I did like gin. It made me a better dancer, for a start. I began to absorb the alcohol the moment it hit my lips.

'This is nice.'

'I got you a double, to get you in a party mood. And it's quite a fight for a little lady like you to get to the bar.'

'We don't usually have to buy drinks for ourselves, do we, Jill?' What possessed me to say that? Billy played along with it but he wasn't fooled. He could see I was ready to be charmed (or corrupted, my mother would have said), by any handsome man. He had arrived just at the right moment.

Jill stood holding handbags and watching drinks while I danced most of the night with Billy. Any guilt about deserting her soon disappeared when a few boys came over and talked to her. Walter was among them, I think. When the last slow dances came on, Billy whispered in my ear, seducing me more effectively than any of the other physical approaches taking place around the room. I watched as the girls pulled their partner's slithering hands into more respectable places. I closed my eyes as Billy told me what I wanted to hear.

Jill appeared philosophical about me winning Billy.

'He's only here for the summer; it's hardly worth it – well, for me.' She wrinkled her nose and inspected herself in the mirror, to show how unconcerned she was.

'He's gorgeous though, isn't he? Even if it is only for one summer,' I said. Of course, in my mind it was not for summer.

Jill slipped me a Trebor mint as we sat in the car. Whether it was to disguise my breath from my parents or prepare me for a kiss, I didn't know. It was the kiss that I cared about. Jill's brother was drunk, but pretending sobriety, so he took more care as he drove us home. I sat in the front seat on Billy's knee. Billy would hold me tight, he told me.

*

After the first meeting at the dance, we spent every moment we could together. I had finished my exams and was released from school. Billy was helping on his cousin's farm and not free until five. Instead of lying in bed until noon which I would have liked, I woke early and helped my parents so there was no excuse for their trying to keep me in. I must have been a joy to be around, as glad as Pollyanna. Shirley too, was easy to get along with that summer as she was going through a holy phase. But my parents were always suspicious of too much happiness and in this case they were right.

My father said nothing directly to me but I heard their conversation in the kitchen one evening as I floated past on the way to phone my sweetheart.

'Will you talk to her, Anna? '

'There's no point in talking to her, she won't listen. It's all "Billy this" and "Billy that". Far too serious. '

'I don't trust him.'

'Well, we know nothing about him or his people – he might be a good young fella for all we know. But it's the not knowing, isn't it?'

'I don't need to know his whole breed, seed and generation. I have the measure of him.'

'And?'

'He's as slippery as get out. All that "yes sir, good to meet you sir". Sleeked wee git.'

'But what can we do?' There was a pause, 'Maureen, is that you in the hall?'

Perhaps my feet touched the ground for a moment, for my mother heard me and the conversation stopped.

The next day she tried to have a serious talk with me, but I was eighteen. What did she know? The conversation was good-natured. I had become the perfect daughter.

'Maureen, I think you need to catch yourself on and not spend all your time with that Billy fella.'

'I'm not spending all my time with him. Will I fold those for you? You sit down.' I gently guided my mother to the armchair that sat in the corner of the kitchen and started folding the washing. 'I need to help more, now that the exams are over. Will I make you a wee cup of tea?'

My mother was flummoxed but persevered, talking vaguely about 'being careful' and 'having respect for yourself'.

'I do respect myself. He respects me. You should be happy.' I leaned over and kissed her playfully. 'You shouldn't worry. You'll give yourself wrinkles.'

'I'm sure he's a nice young man, but he's still a man. We don't know anything about him. Be careful. Go out in a crowd. Don't be forgetting about your friends. He's only here for the summer.'

'All the more reason to enjoy every minute of it. It's better than going out with some boring culchie who's never been further than Ballymena. Right, I'm off to get in the bath.' I skipped up the stairs, untainted by my mother's caution. Life was great.

Billy was cunning. For weeks he made no demands. Compared to other boys he was so easy to be with. I didn't have to keep saying no, but Billy had tactics when it came to girls. He was a bit older than me and the difference of him being American and a visitor gave him some sort of power over me. Over and above the power that boys had over girls in those days –

and probably still have. He started to tell me how much he loved me and desired me. He would talk in great detail about what he would like to do with me but obviously couldn't because of how much he respected me. All of that was much more enticing than any clumsy groping. Those kisses. That talk.

Looking back, I can see how he reeled me in. He pretended to be very understanding of my over-controlling family. Telling me I needed to get away and that I shouldn't let them hold me back. So understanding, so nice and then suddenly so manipulative. He isolated me from my friends by saying he could see I found them childish and that I was better than them. I was going to go places. He told me what I wanted to hear. Within the space of a month I was avoiding friends' phone calls and later, I avoided my friends altogether because he didn't like me seeing them. He loved me so much, you see. He couldn't bear to be parted from me.

In the end, I didn't want them to see me with him because I didn't want them to see how he was treating me. Sly put-downs of how I could be real pretty if I lost some weight, or mentioning that American girls put a higher priority on grooming but then I couldn't be expected to have the time, living on a farm. So from feeling confident and excited and full of joy I began to look in the mirror for the flaws he had helpfully pointed out for future improvement. I felt he was losing interest so I tried my best to hang on to him – and that involved going further. He talked about things like 'making out 'and 'third base' which I didn't really follow but I knew I needed to give him more.

The more I gave him, the more the rules became his. He told me I needed to understand that I couldn't just say no any time I wanted. It was hard for men to stop if the girl had made them too excited. He implied it was harmful or dangerous even. I imagined some sort of explosion. Nothing was happening at my pace and I couldn't talk to Jill as she was fed up that I was ignoring her. In the end, he said I owed him. I had let him pay for all the petrol. I'd led him on – and if I loved him I would do it. I suppose I thought he was right. I must love him, as I'd let him see me naked and by then we'd gone to various bases that I didn't fully understand. So one day, I gave in.

'Okay. We'll do it tomorrow,' I said and he was so pleased and loving and gentle that I thought I'd done the right thing.

'If you're sure, honey. You have no idea how happy that would make me. But only if you're sure.'

I was sure. I was really sure.

The sex was of course a disaster – well, for me anyway. Any desire I had had disappeared through nerves and the fact that he had undermined me so successfully over the past few weeks.

'I didn't think you'd do it,' he said afterwards. He was triumphant, and if there had been a bedpost around he would have put a notch in it but we were in his cousin's car with the seats back and covered by a blanket that smelled of animals. My skin stuck to the seat after a while so that as he moved on top of me there was a sensation not unlike pulling off Elastoplast. That is my most acute memory of the night I lost my virginity.

I woke up one day and felt altered. Everything tasted different. My head felt light but there was a heaviness about the whole of the rest of my body. Billy had assured me that it was impossible to get pregnant the first time, but no periods came. I didn't really need the private doctor's appointment, which my mother organised in Belfast when she finally guessed. I had been trying for weeks to find the words to tell them. There was always a crowd round the place for the potato gathering. I couldn't tell my dad, but on the other hand I didn't want to tell my mother without him around to calm her down. Each morning the realisation of what I had to face up to lurched into my consciousness before my eyes opened. It was never the right time to tell them.

In the end it was my mother who brought it into the open.

'I don't fancy salmon,' I said.

'Well, take an egg sandwich then.' My mother liked us to eat.

'I'm okay. I'll have toast.' As I walked to the toaster my mother watched me.

'Are you on some sort of toast-only diet, Maureen? That's all you eat these days,' said Shirley.

When Shirley went through to the front room, instead of turning *The Archers* on, my mother sat down opposite me.

'What?' I said.

'You know what, don't you?'

My hand went to my stomach.

'You stupid girl. How can I tell your father?' She sat there with her head in her hands for so long I could not bear it. I didn't know what she was going to do next. 'Out of my sight,' she said.

I went to my room and sat looking out of the window until the darkness came and I could see my reflection in the glass staring back at me accusingly. I got under the bedclothes and lay waiting.

Nothing happened until morning.

'Get up, we're going to Belfast.' My mother put a small tray with a cup of tea and the toasted heel of a loaf beside me. I don't believe this was an act of kindness. It was to keep me out of the way. I got up and put on a sombre-looking dress. It was already pulling tight across the bust. I sat waiting in my room until she came to get me. My father was in the car. The engine was running.

'He knows.' Those were the only words said to me on the journey. They discussed the weather, the traffic and all the building going on. I sat in the back with a plastic bag in my hand, concentrating on not vomiting. From that day until the day I left for Glasgow, my mother barely spoke to me. No wonder I thrived in the unwed mothers' home.

When Agnes first went into labour, she said she didn't know

what all the fuss was about. The staff told her it wasn't proper labour yet and told her to rest. She came into my bed and all night I felt her tightening womb against my back. After breakfast I returned to my room and her labour had really started. Agnes had changed from a giggling little girl just turned fifteen into some sort of crazy woman, rocking backwards and forwards, grasping and gripping at things as if trying to stop herself being sucked away. Her nightie was already clinging to her and her hair hung round her face like strands of tinned spaghetti.

'Before the next one, you'll have to let go of me and we'll walk downstairs. Come on, it'll be over soon, dear.' The Green Grove nurse eased her apron from Agnes's grip and helped her up. 'We're going downstairs now. If we get moving we'll be there before the next one starts. Off we go.'

I started to follow them out of the room but the nurse turned to me.

'You stay there, Maureen. You stay out of the way.'

Agnes didn't even bother to turn to say goodbye to me. I didn't understand. I lay crying on the bed and couldn't face the morning walk. Later that day I found a folded bit of paper in my shoe. I opened it and inside was a large lock of her hair and a note.

For the attention of Miss Maureen Hammond

Dear Mo, my new but true friend,
If I die, please give this to Andy and write to tell him I loved him very much. You will find his address on the letter in the pocket of my suitcase. I liked sharing a room with you even though I thought I wouldn't.
Your friend for ever
Agnes Sarah Ramsay-Del Mar
PS. Half the hair is for my baby if it survives.

PPS. You can keep a bit of my hair for yourself if you want.
PPPS. There is some shortbread from my Auntie Marjorie in a wee tin in the top drawer. You can have it.

*

I still have that note. I didn't need to keep the lock of hair because Agnes Sarah Ramsey – 'Del Mar' – survived. She is now Agnes Brown and Andy has a chain of butcher's shops. She sends a card and a long letter every Christmas, and in the early days she enclosed a photo of Rory, the red-haired baby that preceded their marriage by one year. Now there are grandchildren. Most years she calls me on my first baby's birthday and mainly listens to me cry.

*

The nurse called Tanya comes over because she sees that I am crying. I haven't cried for years about that time. Tanya is sitting on the bed, her one arm resting on my walking frame and the other holding my bad hand, automatically unfolding my fingers and straightening them. I wonder would my mother have relented like Agnes's did if they had seen the baby, that little mewing grabbing creature that searched for milk along my chest. So perfect and so precious. Precious to another mother now. I feel a pain in my heart. Tanya hands me a plastic glass of lukewarm water. Somehow it calms me as if it had been a swig of whiskey.

'Tea?' asks Tanya, the cure-all in this country.

I shake my head, murmur a negative sound and try to smile. Even tea won't make this better.

'That was nearly a "no". You're coming on. Soon we'll be

getting all kind of chat from you. I'll be doing my case study at the weekend so I want to sit in on your speech therapy,' she looks over her shoulder, 'if Sister will let me out of here.'

14

When I'm due for the speech therapy, Tanya appears even though she has not been on the ward this morning. She has come in early to see how I am doing. I am a little uneasy about someone from the ward coming with me. They must get reports up here, but they seem unaware of my progress, speech-wise. We decide to walk the whole way there, with the promise of a wheelchair back if I need it.

'Well, how's about you, Maureen?' says the speech therapist kindly, as I manoeuvre myself onto a chair. Tanya stands around, unsure of whether to help.

'You take a seat there, Nurse love, and then we'll get started on a wee bit o' hard work. She's a great wee woman here, doing well – aren't ya?' Mandy, the buttery speech therapist, settles in a chair, pouts and starts on my vocal exercises. Her lazy Belfast slang is now suddenly upgraded into newscaster English solely for the purposes of her profession. 'Have you been practising the exercises up in the ward?'

'Umm,' I mutter like a sulky teenager. I shake my head in case she hasn't got it.

'Don't be self-conscious about having a go. It will get better. Confidence is a big part of it. No one will judge you.'

We go through the programme of work that she has prepared for me. When we start practising the waa waa type sounds, I decide I'll try the singing again.

'Waa Waa One, two, three, four, five, once I caught a fish alive.' My voice gains strength and I have another go. 'One, two, three, four, five, once I caught a fish alive.'

'Well, that's grand, Maureen. It's a singing teacher you're

needing and I'm tone deaf.' She turns to Tanya. 'What's next in the song?'

'Six, seven, eight, nine, ten, then I let it go again,' Tanya sings out.

I try to copy her but can't get past ten.

'We could ask her sister what her favourite songs were.' Tanya is enthusiastic.

I shake my head.

'Not keen? Well, we'll leave it a wee while.' The speech therapist has picked up my reluctance to involve the family. 'You can help her back up on the ward, Nurse.'

When we are finished, Tanya wheels me back on a big awkward chair.

"You must be pleased. It's coming back, isn't it? What ward are you in?'

'One, two, three.'

She stops the wheelchair in a quiet alcove at the entrance to ward three and sits on a chair beside me.

'Not being able to talk at all can be a relief for a while, I suppose. You can put your life on hold. Less pressure. Questions and all that.'

I nod and feel sad. It's true. I have enjoyed being suspended in silence and not having to answer to anyone – quite literally. We go back to the ward and the lunch and rest routine.

*

Shirley has brought some photos in today. She waves them too close and too quickly in front of my nose. Is this some sort of therapy? If so, it's pretty frantic.

'Look, there's you and Walter – and which dog is that? Is it Blackie? No, it's Rover.'

Walter would have called all the dogs by the same name if he had his way. Jackie and Claire tried to insist on 'Fluffycoat' or 'Princess' but these dogs were working members of Team McCormack, and most of them were called Rover.

I remember the photo well, even if I only get a glimpse of it today. It was taken one Easter. There are crocuses in 'the cauldron' as Shirley and I used to call the old black pot by the back door. The dog was a pup and we were keeping it away from the sheep until it settled a bit. In the picture I am sitting on my hunkers and Walter is standing behind me, looking down. We were all in the same team then. That day, nine lambs had arrived. I am looking great, even though I had had very little sleep, hair blowing halfway across my face, looking directly at the dog as if we were sharing a joke. I am wearing a pair of Walter's dungarees together with a white lacy blouse. Even though the photo is in black and white I can tell I had my bright red lipstick on.

The next picture, taken years before, is a formal photo of Shirley and me dressed for church. We are wearing the hairy coats which smelled like dog baskets when wet. We have had our hair painfully sculpted into ringlets so it must have been a special occasion. In church we sent each other messages by writing words with fingertips on the palms of each other's hands. Short messages like 'I need a pee' or 'church is boring'. We sat, smiling sisters appearing to hold hands, bizarrely giving each other mischievous looks when we could legitimately say 'Jesus Christ' without getting a clip round the ear.

Church was a serious business for our family. My mother and father are in the picture. He looks as if he has the wrong body for his head. Apparently when I was a wee girl I didn't recognise him when he had a suit on and used to ask for the other daddy. Father didn't always go to church. There was often some animal-related emergency which seemed to resolve very quickly, as by the time we got back he was reading *Farmer's Weekly* and drinking tea in the kitchen. I didn't know if my mother colluded with this. Perhaps she worried that if we thought church was optional she'd never get us there again.

Shirley hands me the next picture,

'Walter was a bit funny about the camera, wasn't he? Did he not like his photograph being taken?'

She must remember something of the atmosphere that Christmas. Mother wanting everything cleared up in time for The Queen, and Billy Smart's Circus on the telly. Meticulous folding of used wrapping paper and the ritual packing away of the good knives and forks were as much part of Christmas as Santa and the turkey. Claire and Jackie were in the yard pushing doll's prams – Jackie in a pink nightie on over her clothes and Claire wearing oven gloves, Shirley's Christmas present for our mother. Shirley wanted a picture. The prams had been sent by our auntie who lived in England.

'Walter, you take it – I'll get the kettle on.' Shirley handed the camera over to him and he headed to the door. 'Take a few, then we can send one to Auntie Helen with the thank you letter.'

I watched him moving round the girls to get a good background. Mother was always cross if we got the manure heap in the picture. I went to the window and made a swirling motion with my finger to ask him to get the girls to turn round, but he came in without taking another picture.

'You should have got them to turn round to face you.'

'I didn't want to disturb them. They're playing.'

I knew what this was really about. From a distance they looked like two perfect little girls. He never wanted Jackie's face captured close up. He wanted the child we had never had, but lost.

I went out to call the girls in. The sky hung grey like sodden cotton wool.

'Come on, girls, run to the door. You must be freezing, Come and have a bear hug.' I gave a roar and chased them in.

In the kitchen I could hear my mother complaining, 'She'll get them all excited. They've both been up since the scrake of dawn. By bedtime they'll be overwrought.'

'It's Christmas Day, for goodness sake,' I said.

'Jackie will not sleep if you get her up to "high doh". You know what she's like.'

Even now, Jackie will say 'don't waste film' when she sees the camera out. Walter hated the idea of having more and more images of Jackie's face.

We seldom had the appetite for arguing, but there was one time when I had had enough.

'You'll use up the whole film,' he said.

'I bought it.'

'You've taken a dozen pictures already.'

'But probably only one picture will turn out any good.'

'Well, take a bit of time over it and you might get better pictures. Instead of just clicking the camera at anything.'

'I'm clicking *at my daughter*.' My voice became tight and furious.

I was near the end of the film anyway and I rewound it in a temper and flung the camera at him. Not to catch, but to hurt. It hit his shoulder and he caught it by the strap.

'Here, take it,' I said. 'I've had enough, so I have. I'll get my own camera and film.'

'There was no call for that. I only...'

'I've had enough, I said!'

After that, taking pictures was never a neutral activity. I was always the one who stuck them in the photo album and for a while there were no pictures of Walter in it as a protest. But Jackie noticed, and since the album was mainly for her, I relented. I honestly don't think Walter could have picked Jackie out of an identity parade of people with Down's Syndrome, so little did he study her face.

It's funny how no one ever said Jackie took after me or mentioned any family resemblance. The genetic plan for my child laid down one extra copy of a chromosome 21- but the genetic material is all from Walter and me, regardless of the Down's. She was one of us, I could see that. But even the most sympathetic and the thoughtful didn't say, 'She has your smile, Maureen,' or 'Her hair's the same colour as yours, Walter.' Perhaps they subconsciously thought it was an insult to mention any resemblance to the girl with the extra chromosome.

Claire arrives. She has a way of making an entrance that almost demands applause. Claire is taller than both her mum and dad. She has a mouth and a smile made for lipstick, and eyebrows that would meet in the middle if not groomed. This gave her a frowny accusatory look when a child, but she has grown into them. She is big on accessories and without them she looks like a Christmas tree waiting for decoration. Claire always seems to be 'going through a phase'. Shirley has been saying this ruefully almost since her daughter was born. Claire is forgetfully kind, always meaning to do things. She loves Jackie fiercely and I sometimes think it is Jackie she returns home to see rather than her parents. She has higher expectations of her cousin than the rest of us do, and Jackie responds well to this. Jackie has a way of 'helping' which involves walking round the kitchen and moving things slightly to give the illusion of busyness without actually contributing. Claire will have none of that.

I have been too soft and inconsistent, I can see that now. Walter and I should have pushed our Jackie more, but it seemed too much of a struggle. I hated it when she was angry with me. I just wanted her to love me. Perhaps it suited me to keep her as a little girl who loved me unconditionally because I felt my marriage was missing something. Another reason to lie here feeling guilty.

Claire has come to relieve her mum, who has to get back to the shop this afternoon.

'Oh, let me see.' Claire reaches for the pictures.

'Here, I'll leave them. I'd better get back or your dad'll give off. He has some man to see.' Shirley flurries out, leaving a trail of instructions behind her.

'I love old photos,' Claire says comfortably. 'Oh I remember that Christmas, with the new prams. Remember the way we used to try to get the cats to sit in them?' She turns the picture of me and Walter towards me. 'What age were you then, you and Uncle Walter? Not much older than me, I reckon. You look like a Land Girl in this one. You look really happy, both of you.'

'Yes.'

'Mum said you were a proper little perfect wife in the early days. Make-up on and dinner on the table for your man. Maybe it wore off?'

'Yes.'

'To be honest, you never seemed that... well-suited to me. Not that happy. I wondered was it Jackie that sort of changed things?'

I shook my head.

'I mean the strain of looking after her and all that?'

Again I shook my head.

'So you just grew apart or something?'

I shrugged.

'It's a shame. You seemed to hold each other back. As if you were badly cast in a play together.' Claire goes on to talk about plays she's seen and been in where the casting hasn't worked. She's good at telling stories. Often I haven't the time to listen, but today she is on great form and the rest of the afternoon passes very quickly. She switches again to the photo.

'The reason I ask about the photo is... I've been thinking about how you actually know whether someone is right for you. Do you have the definite feeling that he's "the one" or do you think, "We get on okay, he'll do. I've got to that age"? I don't know. I don't want to be too fussy. But I know that even though my dad is an eejit, my mum still loves him – but Uncle Walter was a good man and you didn't seem... Well, I don't know, I wonder did you love him?'

I tilt my horizontal hand from side to side and try to look equivocal to signify that I can't give a definitive answer. I hardly know myself. It wouldn't be the sort of love a girl like Claire would be looking for now. I know that much.

'But you stayed with him. You could have split up when times were tough. Sorry, maybe it's upsetting but I'm interested because I'm trying to decide something. Why did you stay together?'

I cannot answer – and even if I could speak I don't know how I could explain to someone of her generation.

'Or he could have left you, even?'

Until she said that, it had never even occurred to me that he might have left me. I couldn't imagine him ever telling me he'd had enough or he was bored or had met someone else. Where would he have gone? What would he have done? Here's me thinking I was trapped, but Walter could hardly have left me even if he wanted to. The house and the farm were bequeathed to me by my parents. I never put Walter's name on the deeds. I could have said, 'Goodbye, off you go, pack your bags' – and he would have been left with no job, no home. He didn't leave a will. There was no need: he had nothing to call his own. We had a joint bank account. When he died, they sent me a new cheque-book without his name on it. That was the only financial disruption. Imagine if he had done that to me, kept me dependent? I thought about it a lot in the months after his death. Did he see it as a vote of no confidence in our marriage, perhaps? Looking back on it, it was a terrible thing to do to a man. To anyone.

Claire is flicking through a magazine. She stops and looks around the ward.

'I've told my agent I'm doing research here. I'm trying to get another part on *Casualty*, with luck it'll be someone conscious this time. The trick is to catch their attention enough in a small part so that you get a regular part. But if you are too memorable in the patient role you can never get upgraded to staff in case viewers remember you.' She looks at me to check I am listening. 'Are you okay here?'

'Yes.'

'It must be weird not knowing what's going to be happening. In limbo. I feel like that a lot of the time myself. You know – waiting around for things to happen. I can't make decisions any more. I think that's why I'm not sure about this boyfriend. He's got a job in Edinburgh. He's asked me if I want to join him there. I'm very used to travelling for any work that I can get, but this time I don't know whether I can make the decision. I need him to say, "You have a permanent part in a soap called *Our Relationship*, set in Edinburgh, and then I'd find it easy. Oh I don't know.'

She runs her hands through her hair and sighs. 'Is it worse to regret something that you do or something that you don't do?'

I shrug. There is no answer to this. My regrets are split evenly between the two, I think.

'I wish I'd asked you loads of stuff when I could. I think you're a wise woman, Auntie Maureen.'

I laugh. Sounds almost normal too. I am the last person who can give this girl advice. I missed the adventure of a place in art college by getting pregnant. My time at teacher training college feels like a film I half-remember. My parents had hoped I'd go to Stranmillis in Belfast so they could keep an eye on me, but I rebelled. I needed out. I didn't want to come home every weekend and hang about at the same YFC dances drinking squash and eating dry sandwiches as if nothing had happened.

But in reality life in the London suburbs dragged too, not living up to my teenage dreams of art college and wearing berets and drinking black coffee across the table from pale intellectual men in Bohemian cafés. I had gone to teacher training college to get as far away from home as possible – and then ended up back where I started, marrying exactly the sort of man my parents would have picked if they'd organised it themselves.

Follow your dreams. Don't follow your dreams. What a choice! But I wouldn't want anyone to think my life had been a complete disaster. There has been a lot of joy. Friends, Jackie, school, the kids there, banter in the staff room. Sitting here in hospital, I am dwelling on the regrets too much. Too much time. It never suited me...

*

There had to be an inquest after Walter's death. I felt accused somehow but it was only because it had come out of the blue. In a crowd of men his age you'd have picked Walter out as the man least likely to die early. Aged fifty, he was wiry, drank less in a year than a lot of fellows drink in a night. He'd never smoked. They found in the end it was some sort of an aneurism.

Tom Kelso came to talk to me about it.

'It was a time-bomb ticking away. I couldn't have picked it up even if he had ever come to see me,' he told me.

'I know, Tom. I know.'

'How's Jackie? How's she taken it?'

'She's enjoying the attention. All the visitors, you know.'

'He was well-respected.'

It was true, Walter was well-respected. Respected rather than loved, I think, which would have pleased him more. I had a lot to think about, whole areas of responsibility I had devolved to him.

The funeral came a few days later. The slow walk down the lane with George, the McGovern brothers and several cousins taking it in turn to lift the coffin. There was something bleak and prehistoric about the scene. You could imagine you were back in the time when we built dolmens and cairns for our dead. The same sort of ritual. Men carrying one of their own aloft on his final journey.

Jackie and I held hands and stood by the door, watching until the undertaker led us to the car. On the way to the church there were people waiting at the end of lanes. Half the townland followed in cars specially cleaned for the occasion. Jackie wanted to wave and Shirley wouldn't let her.

It was a long hard day. At the church, there were murmured condolences, Jackie sat with Claire in a distant pew so I felt alone and unprotected at the front of the church, not like at my mother and father's funerals with Walter by my side. After the service, Shirley was with me, her hand on my arm to steer and perhaps to comfort me. There were second cousins I hadn't seen for years. I wouldn't have recognised them if they'd passed me in the street but here they were, looking unreal, like kids in a school play, made up to look older.

The day was a blur, strangely like my wedding day, ushered around, no time to speak to anyone. The uncoupling after all these years. People came back to the house. There were sandwiches and cakes on every surface in the kitchen, Claire touring with a teapot and a jug of milk and George with a bottle of Black Bush. And as distant relatives went back home and locals retired to do the milking, the house began to clear. I found Jackie in our room hugging Walter's pyjama top and we both lay in the bed crying, while downstairs, Shirley and Claire reunited Tupperware boxes with their owners and found people's coats in the cupboard under the stairs.

Tom and Elizabeth Kelso had come to the house. Elizabeth

had never been inside before. Even in my confused state I could imagine her sizing the place up, thinking the sitting room could do with a lick of paint.

'We're going to go, Maureen,' she said after about twenty minutes. 'Tom's got surgery this evening. You look tired. We'll leave you with your family and friends.'

I nodded and tears came to my eyes. Intended or not, I felt it was a snub. 'We're no friends of yours' was what I took from that.

Elizabeth got in the car and there was a fuss while Tom located who was blocking them in. He came over to me before he left.

'We're away, Maureen, but I'll... Well, we'll all be thinking of you,' he said, aware he was being watched. I hadn't the heart to read any message into what he said. I was so full of guilt and grief.

The house and the yard cleared and Jackie and I came downstairs and sat with Shirley, George and Claire watching *Birds of a Feather*.

'That Elizabeth Kelso's an uptight madam,' George commented. 'She needs a good...'

'Stop!' shouted Shirley and Claire together.

'Stop your nonsense, George,' said Jackie.

We all laughed.

'You've heard that a fair few times, Jackie,' said Shirley.

'But you know what I mean,' said George.

'She wouldn't touch a thing. "I *never* eat between meals".' Shirley put on Elizabeth's voice, posh Dublin with added elocution.

Shirley was sensitive about her natural roundness now merging with middle-age spread. The running down of Elizabeth turned into more widespread and good-natured comments on how old or how young, how fat or how thin the cousins were.

When the other two left, Jackie and I were alone.

'Daddy's not coming back.'

'No, love.'

'He's in heaven. Is it true?'

'Well, if anyone's going to heaven, it's your dad.'

Jackie smiled. 'It's true.'

'Yes, love, it's true,' I said quietly.

That night, I wore Walter's pyjamas and tried to soak up the last of him. I was closer to him that night than I'd been for a long time, but maybe that's always the way.

*

I went back to work almost straight away – getting up early and working late into the night when I got home. I couldn't sit still, couldn't read, couldn't bear the radio on. Weekend days were long. Jackie and I would sometimes go to a café on the coast road and sit looking at the sea and eating stale Paris buns. Jackie, picking sugar lumps up with tongs and dropping them into her mouth, was amazed she wasn't getting told off. When trying to pack away this grief, I opened the compartment in which I had contained the other. I thought again of Glasgow and Jackie's unknown older sibling.

*

I'd stayed at Green Grove until I was pronounced fit to travel. I'd said goodbye to my baby in the office of the Home two days after the birth. In the background the clerk was waving the recently signed adoption papers to dry the ink as if to make the arrangement even more irreversible.

'Baby will be going to its new family after a check-up. We tell the girls not to look out of the window for the remainder of the day.'

The softness of my baby's skin was unbearable. Its touch against mine, like an ice burn. I could feel the tingle of milk coming in again even though they'd been dosing me with tablets and binding my chest.

'We know this is hard. In five minutes, Baby will be taken out of that door and you'll be taken through the hall. Five minutes. We've worked out what's the easiest way for everyone.'

They fussed around the paperwork like extras in a film. I sat on a brocade nursing chair just looking at my baby. Trying to learn that little face. My heart broke that day. I'm not sure it's been repaired yet. There'd been letters and phone calls from Mother over the past weeks. She said she was glad the ordeal was nearly over. *We'll put it all behind us. You'll be very welcome back home. Sure, this was the only way, wasn't it?* Unsaid was, 'Don't you change your mind. There'll be no welcome if you come back with a baby.'

Miss McKenzie walked me to my room and rocked me in the big chunky arms that had rocked a hundred mission babies. She told me stories of idyllic adoptive families and happy children, but at that time I did not want my child to be happy without me. Miss McKenzie suggested playing draughts or gardening. She was at her wits' end and teary herself. She saw my water-colours and paper.

'Why don't you do a wee painting?' she suggested. 'We could do with something nice on the walls. How about the view out the window? I'll sit with you.'

So I painted a picture of the trees in the Green Grove garden and the sundial and the path where we girls had our walks. Along the path I painted in the same grey-stone tones a message: *You were loved.*

'Can it go with my baby?' I sobbed.

'If it'll stop you crying, my dear,' said Miss McKenzie. She handed me a replacement hanky and looked at the picture. 'It's lovely, dear. I'm sure it will be treasured. I'll take it down now quickly, in case... I'll just take it down.'

That night, they let Agnes back to visit me. Miss McKenzie minded her baby downstairs. They normally separated the girls who kept their babies from the ones who 'decided to give their baby a better chance' as they called it. Agnes had a quarter bottle of whiskey with her, wrapped in a clean nappy. We had it in hot milk and we talked as I struggled to cope with that grief. That was the last time I saw Agnes.

15

Sister is on the ward today so everything's ship-shape. The beds have to be made before the doctors come round. Tanya's on duty. She brings me a Walkman, a nursery-rhyme tape and a recording of some Beatles songs.

'It's not patronising, is it? I thought it might help – you know, some familiar songs. I can get it back when you're going home.' So she plugs me into 'Baa Baa, Black Sheep' and 'Hickory, Dickory Dock' and goes about her business. The doctors come around and I take the headphones off. There's not such a band of them here as in the other hospital, and they are more aware of us as people. People their mother might know, people they might bump into in the Spar some day.

'So you're doing well, Mrs McCormack. Mandy the speech therapist says there's a bit of progress too. It's a slow old business but once we get you well on your feet, you'll be able to be off. There's only you at home?'

'And the daughter – you know,' says the Ward Sister, trying to signal with her eyes.

'Oh yes, the daughter. Have we organised an assessment?'

I want to ask what this is all about. I want to say I'll manage, that Shirley will help me, that Jackie is no trouble – but I don't know if any of that is true.

'OT assessment is organised for...' Sister flicks through the notes, 'today actually.'

They walk on to the next patient. I am nervous about what the OT will say. It feels like an exam, a driving test for my new body. The OT has already seen me in action, given me tips for getting dressed, taken me to a deserted kitchen where I made a cup of tea I wasn't given time to drink.

Tanya returns and starts rummaging in the locker. 'Have you got a jacket? No, you probably don't.'

For a moment I think that Tanya is organising my escape.

'Where's your shoes? Umm, nice trainers.'

Claire bought them for me to go with the tracksuit. Velcro fastenings which I can manage myself. Jackie and I now both have good reason to thank Mr Velcro, if he exists, for his great invention. To get Tanya's attention, I try to speak. I won't be able to say what I want, so any sound will do.

'One potato, two potato, three potato, four,' I sing.

'Brilliant,' says Tanya. 'It worked.' She is so thrilled with my singing that it's hard to get her to focus on what I am trying to find out. I point to the door and draw a question mark on the corner of a newspaper.

'They didn't tell you about the OT assessment? They're taking you on a home visit to see how you will get on after discharge.'

I needed warning for that. It takes me longer to prepare for things both physically and emotionally than it did before. I wonder what it will feel like to go home. I don't know how long it has been. I've tried to count the days as they pass, like a prisoner, but I don't know when my sentence will end or even when it began.

We approach the farm slowly. The OT is driving me herself, with a student map-reading. She's a nervous driver, she tells me, but has never had an accident. We stop at the top of Stavey Brae to look at the map yet again. I could easily point the way for them, but they haven't asked me and I want to enjoy the view without the pressure of getting them there. Although I often felt trapped by this place, I know that the farm is a big part of me. I feel I could lift sections of the view, like flaps in a child's book, and find a bit of my story underneath. A few leafless deciduous trees have won a battle for their place among the pines. Through gaps in the treeline, I can see the lake that Jim and I swam in.

From the middle of the lake you get a different view. Until the day of the first swim I had never seen the hill or those trees from there before. Maybe no one had. People round here don't swim for pleasure. Well, there isn't usually the weather for it. Yet here I was, swimming in my slip. I turned over in the water, like a seal doing a trick, just for the love of it. When I turned upwards I saw green-blue-green flash past. Grass-sky-trees.

I started to swim slowly towards the far end of the lake. To look at it you'd think it would take no time but I swam and swam and still had a quarter of the lake to go. I turned towards the sun to go back and with the pine trees and the high flat meadow silhouetted, the place looked alpine. The red Massey Ferguson tractor with its old sacking seat cover was parked where the lane met the meadow. The grass was uncut and there were seeding flowers poking out over the top of it.

I got near the shore. Jim was starting to struggle out. I floated on my back, eyes shut, to spare his dignity as he scrambled. When my eyes opened he was standing there, wiping himself down with his shirt.

'It's freezing,' he shuddered. 'How can you stay in for so long?'

'I'm not skinny like you – it has its advantages. I've never swum in such still water. It's so clear, isn't it?'

'Wait till you try coming out.'

When I felt the muddy edge, I tried to glide horizontally for as long as I could. The weeds and itchy moving things ribbed against me and I had to stand. The muddy bed sucked me right down, about six inches. I walked out like a toddler in new shoes, squealing in mock disgust at the gloopy feel and the clouds of underwater dust. Mud gave way to shallower water, toe–stubbing rocks and layers of midges in the air. I winced on tiptoes, arms out for balance. Jim walked to the water's edge in his unlaced boots and tried an amateur fireman's lift. Over his shoulder, the long thin lake stretched out behind us like a road. I thought about how Walter had seen it as a nuisance, a waste of good farmland, something you had to drive round.

I slipped shivering over Jim's warm chest when we reached the grass where my dress and shoes lay. He took a step back as I landed, but he was still looking at me. One hand was ready to steady me. I felt conscious of my petticoat clinging to me and had to move.

'You have a midge on you,' I said. I moved closer and reached purposefully to wipe his cheek. There was no insect there at all.

'We could lie in the trailer in the sun to get dry. It's cold in the wind. Or do you want to get on?'

'It can wait.' It could wait forever for all I cared.

Jim gave me a leg up and I laid down a couple of meal bags like towels on a beach. He lay on his front beside me. I wished I'd laid the bags closer together.

'Are there fish in there, do you think?' I nodded towards the lake. 'I could certainly feel things moving.'

'What, like that big black leech on your neck there?' he said, reaching over and running his cold finger below my hairline.

'I am not going to be taken in,' I said, laughing. 'Look how relaxed I am.'

'Even if it moves right down your back,' he said, moving his finger.

'Especially if it moves...' and then I didn't feel relaxed at all.

The day had started as normal. Jim arrived at eight every morning and I would pull a brush through my hair and put a bit of lipstick on as I heard his motorbike in the yard. No reason for it, except habit. Jim had been around for years, helping out at farms in the area. He was a young fella. Not married. No one knew much about him but he would appear as if by magic when needed and move from farm to farm when we were getting in the silage or sometimes at lambing. I didn't even know his last name but Shirley had worked out he was not a Protestant. When Walter died, I was left with a working farm, a full-time job and a dependent daughter. There was help from the McGoverns and some cousin of Walter for a few weeks, and then Jim knocked on the door.

'Have you any work for a man with time on his hands?'

'Have you heard?'

'Aye, sorry for your trouble. Walter was one decent man. Do you need a hand? Have you work for me?'

'God, yes Jim. There's too much.' I handed him a cup of tea and he stood by the draining board, rolling a cigarette as I told him what needed doing. We had been working with each other all that summer before the day of the swim. He treated me like a girl his age even though I was half a generation older than him. He would tell me about his travels and people he'd met and drugs he'd tried and hangovers he'd had. He lifted my spirits and I missed him on the days he did not work. He'd never sit and have a cup of tea in the house but would stand near the door of the kitchen. It was as if even to sit down would be to put down roots. He often stayed in an old caravan parked outside the pub when he was in the area, but I offered him the bungalow which was lying empty. At weekends he would still get poured into the caravan after a night at the pub, but most of the time he stayed on the farm.

The day of the first swim, we had been working in the full sun all day, sorting out a bit of fencing and a repair to a wee bridge over the burn that fed the lake. Jackie was in respite care at some great place over the border. I was starting to feel human again, in time to get back to work in September. It was boiling that day in a sun-trap by the lake. The chilled bottles of lemonade I'd packed in a padded bag were now warm and unpleasantly acidic.

'I've had enough. I will never complain about the cold again,' I said as lay down under a tree. 'Leave that, I'll give you a hand in a minute.'

Jim continued gathering up the tools and the jars of nails and took them down to where we'd parked the tractor. He was such a laid-back lad really. He never minded that a woman was telling him what to do. He got on with the work. Although it felt as if that day at the lake came out of nowhere, I suppose it had been building up. Jim was a lovely-looking young fella and there was something about the motorbike and the drifting that made him more attractive, like boys who worked in fairgrounds.

A few weeks before that day I had called round when he was kipping at the caravan. I had to drop his wages off. It was dark outside and he opened the door a few inches and poked his head round. The way the light inside was shining I could see the silhouette of his naked body clearly outlined against the white Formica wardrobe by the door: every hair on his body, every part of him.

'Sorry, I'm not dressed.'

'I know,' I said. 'I'm not coming in. Here's your money.'

I handed the envelope of cash over. I was blushing. I sounded rude. I couldn't get the picture out of my head the whole way home and for a long time after. So, it was in my mind. The idea was there. So did I make the day at the lake happen... ?

*

'Maureen... Maureen. We're here. Were you asleep?'

'Yes.' Was I?

The OT comes round and opens the car door for me and instructs me how to swivel round to get both legs out of the door neatly. The technique reminded me of an article on etiquette Shirley and I had read when we were girls. For several weeks after that we could have been presented at Court, we were so au fait with the manners of the English upper classes.

The way the yard has been concreted, the surface tamped down with planks to give traction in the frost, made it easy to trip. I take the walk to the back door slowly but the ridges in the yard are not the only things that slow me down. At the back door the OT rips open an envelope and there are my keys.

'Right, which one is it? There we go.'

The usually cluttered back porch is swept and clear of bags and boots. The environment is familiar but I am taking another body on a test drive round it. I know about the raised door saddle and the tight corners and I negotiate it with care. The OT looks round the kitchen as if it were a wild landscape she has to tame. The tea–making practice and the long questionnaire we completed at the hospital were just the beginning. Her walking round the kitchen is punctuated with suppressed sighs and subdued tuts. It seems none of my furniture is to be trusted. The microwave sitting on top of the fridge freezer is far too high, the kettle too heavy and the gas cooker should never have been fitted so near a window. Listening to them, you'd think the house was a death trap.

We go through each room; rugs are lifted and rolled, revealing threadbare or stained carpets. There is a lot of measuring. The smell of home, it's hard to describe the essence of it. Shirley has been round dusting so there's an unfamiliar lemon scent over-laying it.

The stairs nearly finish me off and they debate a stair-lift. Should we wait and see, or order one now? There is a downstairs loo so it could be limited to a once-a-day descent and ascent. I'll get stronger, I want to say. I don't want a stair-lift. I am remembering that a man came to measure up for my mother's stair-lift the day of her funeral. We had forgotten to cancel him.

The student is sent to the car for bath accessories. When they are in place, I am observed getting in and out of the bath – fully clothed, of course. My toilet cistern is a very cumbersome design. There is tapping of walls and measuring and lifting of mattresses. Nothing is sacred.

A car drives into the yard. For a second I wonder if it's Walter, but it's coming up to seven years since he died.

'It'll be the sister.' The OT looks at her watch. 'I arranged to meet her at four.'

I hear the back door open.

'It's only me,' shouts Shirley.

'We're upstairs.'

Shirley bounds upstairs. I resent her nimbleness.

'I'm early. I hope you don't mind.'

It feels uncomfortable with four of us in the bedroom, like a badly organised swingers' party.

'She'll need a new bed.'

They run through the list of things I'm going to need. Shirley has brought a small carton of UHT milk and we go down to the kitchen and I make coffee while these three women watch me like parents at a school sports day. I shuffle to the kitchen table to serve them individually. I haven't over-filled the mugs. There is no spillage or scalding. The observers relax. I enjoy drinking from my china mug again. The OT student is still scribbling while we drink our coffee, occasionally getting up to check things. A report will be produced, they tell us, and they begin to pack up their stuff.

Shirley talks to me directly for the first time today.

'Jim's here. He asked if it was all right if he said hello.'

I am not sure about this but I can't say no. Shirley has no idea about our fling.

'Just a quick hello?'

'Yes.'

I tuck the tripod stick behind the chair. Jim comes in, the

blond of summer shorn from his hair but as handsome as I re-member. He's been keeping the farm ticking over since I went into hospital. Most of the fields are let out to a cousin of the Mc-Governs but there are still some sheep to look over and a field or two of potatoes which keeps my hand in.

'It was hard to get in to see you. Too big a queue,' says Jim.

I smile.

'Glad to be home again?'

I smile again. This is torture for him, to be watched by all the others. The student takes some stuff to the car and the OT shows Shirley the bathroom accoutrements. Jim sits down for the first time in my house.

'Are you okay?' he asks.

'So-so.' It's one of my secret repertoire of words, but I don't mind Jim knowing.

'So you didn't see your woman in Belfast?'

'Yes,' I say but look confused. I have no idea what he means.

'She was flying over to see you.'

I look blankly at him.

'Nothing,' he says. 'It'll come back to you. Anyway, Shirley's a character, isn't she?'

He's had to deal with Shirley and that will not have been easy. I wind my finger round and round beside my temple to indicate her craziness. He laughs and leans over and gives me the gentlest dry kiss on the cheek. The kiss you would give a sleeping child. It is an acknowledgement that we mean something to each other.

'I hate hospitals. But I was thinking about you.'

I smile. I would not have expected him to visit. No one knew he'd ever been anything other than someone working for me. It would have felt awkward for him. He stands up and looks round the room, probably surprised at its tidiness. The others come back.

'I'll get on,' says Jim, and goes out to the yard and back to work.

As I slowly and unevenly walk back to the car, I see him tactfully drift off. I am glad he isn't watching. I don't want him to see me as a potential user of a stair-lift. As I get into the car, the OT puts her hand on my head, like they do in police dramas. I give a chuckle but can't explain why.

Jim assumed I would want to have sex. He was only fourteen years younger than me but the shift in attitudes had given everyone different expectations. It was no big deal for him, just something you did. His approach made it easier for me; made me feel it was no big deal either. We'd go about the day's work as if it wasn't on the cards at all and then one or other of us would give in and we'd be all over each other, always somewhere other than the house.

Sometimes he'd say, 'Do you want to come over to the bungalow for a rest?' And we'd go there and I'd sit on the sofa while he unnecessarily put the kettle on and lit a joint, then he'd lie back, head on my lap and smile.

'Have we got time?'

'We've got time.'

We had a pattern where we'd both undress each other and then move together like magnets. The whole time, I was in a state of longing for him; a longing that was not connected to my idea of love but good all the same. I told myself it was more to do with opportunity than anything else. He was so different to Walter. Any emerging stress was smoked away. Occasionally I took a drag on his joint to be sociable and show I wasn't old and disapproving, but to be honest being around him made me calm and happy. I told him he should have been available on prescription. He told me he was. We had a habit of never talking about the here and now. We told stories about the past but never talked of today, us, Walter or anything serious. We certainly never touched the future.

Back on the ward I realise how much the visit home has taken out of me. I need a lot of time to process information. I don't trust my memory. Seeing the house and almost imagining Walter would be there, and then Jim... I can't even remember when we last went to bed together. Was it a year? A month? I am more disorientated than I thought. And I don't know what the time-scale for my leaving hospital is. They'll need time to get their plans in place, I suppose.

It is a relief to be back in the hospital and put everything in suspended animation again. I am tired now but have been shuffling around, helping people find their call bells for the nurse, noticing if their magazine falls to the ground, though not yet able to pick it up for them. It is time I was out of here, I know that, but unless Shirley moves in with me for a while I would not be able to cope at home yet.

I am reading a very gentle novel by Barbara Pym, picked up from the second-hand book rack in the corridor. The novel is not complicated, but it's a struggle. I have to keep referring to the back cover to remember who the characters are.

'That's a good sign. Book in hand. Are you able to concentrate okay?'

For a moment I am irritated. I seem to be more easily irritated now. I want to say that it is hard to concentrate and being interrupted does not help, but I say nothing, of course. It is the Ward Sister with one of the young doctors. They chat at the end of the bed about drugs and measurements and seem pleased.

'And the speech?' asks the doctor.

'Well, the speech therapist is pleased, but you know Mandy, always looking on the bright side. We've not seen a huge difference here on the ward.'

They don't ask me directly and still talk as if I can't hear. They are discussing Mandy, who is apparently a born again Christian. Perhaps she has been praying for me? Well, it hasn't done any harm. They move on to the next bed.

16

Up until now, I haven't minded Shirley rummaging through my stuff and getting the place organised, but today, thinking about my recent visit home, I feel irrationally disgruntled, as if my territory has been invaded. I worry about what Shirley may have found but in reality there won't have been anything that interesting. Perhaps it's a sign I am getting better. Even a couple of days ago I wouldn't have cared about privacy and territory. I thought I'd never see any of it again.

*

When Mother died, we debated when to clear out her stuff. Shirley would have started the day of the funeral but I was more comfortable with my mother's stuff around. In the end we waited for a week or two and attacked it over a Bank Holiday weekend.

Most of the operation was business-like but occasionally, like archaeologists, we'd come across a layer of artefacts that interested us. There were receipts for things that seemed as if they must be in another currency because the prices were so low – undisturbed since the days when you could buy a new kettle for £3 and four pillowslips for £2.50. There was a picture of my father as a young man at the Lammas fair with a bag of dulse or yellow-man, wedding invitations and tickets and programmes. Two envelopes marked *Maureen* and *Shirley*. For a moment I dreamed that they contained profound messages for the pair of us. Each contained a hefty lock of hair, probably from that time when we nearly scalped each other in the cupboard under the stairs. Even in her fury she had knelt on the floor and separated my dark and Shirley's blonder hair into little bunches. We found cuttings about local events, a picture of Walter and my dad at the opening of a new mart. A small notebook of recipes from her mother tied with a brown shoelace. I opened it. My mother's handwriting was almost identical to my grandmother's. We found a label from the cot at the hospital when Shirley was born and two pairs of soft first shoes, unlabelled. A receipt from Green Grove Presbyterian Welfare Society.

'What was that for?' Shirley said. I could talk then, but I kept quiet. Why did she keep that, I wonder? We had no idea of the significance of half the stuff. We cried as we slipped our mother's life into bags destined for charity or for the dump. Despite our resolution to be ruthless, both of us hung onto things that were neither useful, valuable nor beautiful, just because they were our mother's – a shopping list, five buttons off a favourite winter coat, an egg-timer embellished with shells. Shirley and I had pooled our money and brought it back from a Sunday School trip to Portrush. There was a mohair hat that didn't fit either of us but we both wanted it, and a conical metal container for measuring American cups ended up in my kitchen. Memories we didn't know we had.

In a leather writing-case we found a huge bunch of postcards. One from both of us sent when we went away for a week with our auntie to Dublin. The address was written by an adult and the writing side had lines ruled and one sentence: *We have visited* (then a change in handwriting) *a catheedril.* A gushing card of Dingle Bay from me (and supposedly) Walter from our honeymoon in the Free State when we'd stayed in a guest-house by the sea with walls so damp they felt like sponge cake. It had promised the luxury of an ensuite bathroom – which, it turned out, meant there was a plastic concertina door with a magnetic catch between the bedroom and the toilet. I could hardly even pee for the whole week we were there, but in the postcard we were having a grand time. No mention of the mattress with springs that made you feel you were sleeping on a trivet or the fact that Walter wouldn't hold my hand on the beach.

I flicked through other postcards. Claire in Paris writing to her grandma as if she'd be interested in the Pompidou Centre or mime. There are others from me, one marking my arrival in England and another from a second holiday Walter and I took in County Kerry without Jackie. Again the card told nothing of the reality.

*

'Would you look at that?' Walter said.

I turned round to see what had offended him now. It had been a long journey and he was in an irritable mood. A group of scruffy young people were unpacking beach gear from an old bus.

'They're not doing any harm,' I said. I was aware that I had snapped at him, so I went on more gently, 'Though I'm not keen on fair hair in dreadlocks.'

Walter opened the car with the new remote control on his key-ring as if he was firing a laser gun on *Star Trek*.

'I'm going in for a paddle,' I said. 'Are you coming?'

'I'm going to park up there a bit.' Walter got in the driving seat and assumed his driving-the-car position: arms rigid and back firmly against the seat. I was surprised he didn't put his driving gloves on to move the car thirty yards further away from the hippie bus. The tide was out on Inch Strand and I turned to gaze back when I reached halfway to the water's edge. Walter was now safely parked between an Austin Maestro and an elderly couple in a light blue Mini. Neither was near enough to bump doors with him. I was amazed he even brought the new car onto the beach.

The hippie bus was turquoisey blue and must have been fifteen years old, battered like a Matchbox car tumbled about in the bottom of the toy-box. It had been patched with differently coloured side panels and had weird flower-like patterns across the bonnet. Wild-haired children dug holes and piled up drift-wood near the entrance steps. Several pot plants sat along the dashboard. Cactuses; not even Walter could have mistaken them for marijuana. The gang of raggle-taggle children were called into the bus and they drove further down the strand. Were they conscious of Walter moving the car or did they decide to move away from the flask and windbreak brigade? I watched them drive to the end of the beach. Their progress was jerky and slow, as if the Matchbox bus was being pushed by a giant toddler's hand.

Ryan's Daughter was filmed there. I looked at the sweep of the strand, like a golden sandpit that caught the wind so that it was often warmer in the sea than out. I wanted to swim like we did the first time we were there. Walter couldn't be persuaded, and it's lonely swimming on your own. Jackie was in respite care and doing an independent living course. She'd be learning how to use a washing machine, she'd told me. My friends had been keeping me going all week at school about this trip, calling it a second honeymoon and telling me to pack a sexy negligee. I glanced back at the car. Walter was reading yesterday's *Belfast Telegraph*. He always read the small ads though he never bought anything because of fear of being ripped off.

The hippies had left the bus and there was a faint winding of smoke from the sand hills. The children were dragging half a tree towards it and the dad (Walter would laugh at that assump-tion) slipped down a sand hill in his orange shorts to help them. I turned to walk back, this time on the dry sand to warm my feet. Walter spotted my turning and got out of the car to signal me. He'd decided to move the car again.

'Why did you move?' I asked, breathless by the time I reached the car park.

'I saw a parking space and the tide is coming in.'

'But there are fifty cars down there.'

Walter ignored me and I let it go. A convoy of horse-drawn caravans pulled up to park in the field opposite the beach. Shell-suited Germans had replaced Romanies.

'Jackie would love a holiday in one of those,' I said.

Later we headed to the pub for lunch. In the pub car park a farmer was struggling to fit a shovel to an enormous tractor. Walter gave the old man a hand and they got talking. Perhaps Walter misses his tractor, I thought and smiled. I walked on, telling Walter I'd order for him. The sandwiches were already made up but there was a long wait for the glass of Guinness. I was transferring the drinks to the table when Walter came in

'What were you talking about?' I asked.

'Prices.'

'Of tractors?'

'He's a nice aul fella.'

'Are you bored?'

'I'm on my holiday.'

I dismantled Walter's sandwich, took the salad out of it and transferred it into mine. I replaced the top slice of bread and slid the salad-free sandwich towards him.

'Sandwich all right?'

'Yep.'

'Do you fancy a barbecue tonight?' I asked. The cottage we had rented had a sheltered garden with a built-in barbecue.

'Is it worth it for the two of us?'

'You're probably right.' I exhaled with more force than was necessary.

'Did you bring the paper?'

'No, I did not bring the paper.'

Walter wanted to listen to the news on the car radio so we didn't linger over lunch. He took the binoculars out of their case and surveyed the beach from the pub car park.

'Would you look at what those eejits in the bus have done?'

The bus was at the turn of the strand, and from where we were I couldn't tell if it was in the sea already. Walter handed me the binoculars. The waves were washing towards the front tyres.

'Shit. Where have they gone?'

Walter winced at my language and wordlessly he pointed to the shaving of smoke rising from the sand-hills.

'Come on.'

'What's the rush, Maureen? It's up to them. We can't move it.'

'We can warn them. Come on, let's walk up the beach.'

Despite his outward reluctance to help, Walter and I ended up walking faster and faster. Walter stopped for a moment to look through his binoculars and pulled me into towards his chest and put my fingers on the focusing dial so I could look through them. For the first time on the holiday I felt some companionship. We had a shared mission.

When we got near enough to see the spit of foam gathering round the front wheels, I left Walter and ran off in the direction of the campfire. The bus people were lazing round the fire and turning little potatoes on spiked sticks. I shouted from the top of the sand hill and one of the women jumped up, her dark nipple popping out of a sleeping baby's mouth. The men and the children ran over the brow of the hill like children playing cowboys and Indians. By the time the driver and the rest of the entourage had reached the bus I spotted Walter heading back towards our car. The dreadlocked man got into the bus and revved without success. A couple of the other young men placed raffia beach mats under the tyres and ineffectually put their shoulders against it. I held the baby while the women, resigned, started to unpack some things. One of the men sent the children up the beach for buckets of stones, unwilling to admit they were losing the battle. Everyone was damp and grumpy with recriminations. I felt like a visitor arriving in the middle of a family row. I was cross that Walter had walked off.

Suddenly a loud noise drowned out the sound of the sea.

Disorientated, I initially looked towards the sky and then I turned to see Walter and the old farmer from the pub car park speeding towards us in an enormous tractor. The man with dreadlocks walked over towards where the farmer stood, anxious, taking nothing for granted. The farmer sucked air through his teeth and looked grim.

'It's a tricky one. This is a new tractor.' The farmer was a canny Kerryman.

Close up, the bus wheels seemed to be sinking even as we watched them.

'Sixty quid,' the farmer said.

The dreadlocked man looked round to the others. There was silence. No one even bothered to check their wallets.

'Somebody lost a tractor down here last year.' The farmer still wasn't budging.

Walter patted his shirt pocket and said, 'Thirty – if you get it out.'

The farmer nodded.

'Come on.' Walter swung himself up onto the big tractor and picked up a rope. He then jumped down onto the sand again and, leaning on the tractor's large wheel to steady himself, he took off his shoes and socks. He handed his shirt to me and carried the coil of rope into the sea. He stood alone in the water, the backwash running past his legs already at thigh level, and managed to attach the rope to the bus. The group of young people at first appeared mesmerised and then one after another sprang into action. The driver walked into the sea and took the free end of the rope while Walter uncoiled it.

At first the tractor skidded then the bus moved a little and then appeared to slide back even further. Everyone moaned in disappointment.

'Come on – round this side. We have about five minutes or you can say goodbye to your bus.'

Everyone went round to Walter's side and got into position to push. The tyres got a grip and there was a great sucking sound as the bus moved. Walter and the dreadlocked driver fell into the water. Only when they had struggled onto the dry sand, did Walter allow himself a smile.

The farmer went on his way after pocketing Walter's thirty quid.

The hippies were grateful and there was talk of sending us a cheque.

'Come and have something to eat with us. We have fish. Or at least have a drink?' said the mother of the baby.

I looked at my non-existent watch, anticipating Walter's reluctance.

'Maybe we should be getting...'

'We have time for a drink,' said Walter.

We sat side by side with the group round the bonfire. The driver of the bus took a swig from a bottle of wine and handed it to Walter. I watched him to see how he would react. He lifted the bottle to his lips and drank. That moment made the holiday okay.

*

'George is up to something – I know it.' Shirley is barely seated on the plastic hospital chair when she starts. 'Last week he was all for shutting the shop early and going home to bed saying he couldn't wait and would I give him – you know – in the stock room.' Shirley does a hand gesture but her red face has already indicated the nature of what George was suggesting. 'This week we haven't had sex since Sunday. That's *five* days. He says he's tired.'

Five days doesn't seem that long to me but for Shirley it is an unusual and suspicious period of abstinence. My sister looks older and more tired today. The rejuvenating effect of George's attentions is wearing off.

'I can't believe him, Maureen. Just when I need him with Jackie and all that – not that I mind, you know that, he's off helping X move a bookcase and Y with some forms, and delivering a fire-guard to Z. But I'm on to him. I've seen it all before. What do I do? I'm worn out. I do still make an effort.'

Shirley pulls her navy V-neck sweater down to show me a shiny red bra. When she crosses her legs, I can see stocking tops, but all the lingerie in the world will not stop George. It would be like tarting up one of the sheep on the farm for the ram coming round and assuming he would ignore the other ewes. I wish I could do something to restore her dignity. I want to tell her that George's meanderings are not due to any deficiency in her, but rather in him.

17

I am at speech therapy again this morning and the butterball therapist is confused.

'They don't believe me when I say how well you're doing. They say you're still saying nothing. I'm starting to think I'm imagining things.'

We sing 'The wheels on the bus'. I name every day of the week. We play 'I spy'. I can do the I spy with my little eye bit, but the letters take a while and I have to run through the alphabet in a whisper until I get to my chosen letter. When I'm guessing her words, it's hit and miss. I can say 'fluorescent' but not 'light'. As I leave, she comes to help me up but remembers I can do it myself now.

As I leave to journey back to the ward, I am able to say, 'Thank you very much, Mandy.'

She is thrilled.

'Talk to them back on the ward.'

'Yes,' I say, setting off with a spring in my shaky step.

But back on the ward I smile as I wonder how they are going to react when they realise I've been in here all along, listening and taking it all in. I reach my bed and George pops in to see me again with his 'life in the old dog yet' swagger.

'A delivery of clean clothes and toothpaste,' he announces. 'Is there anything else you need?'

He puts a carrier bag on the bed and pulls a chair over. I wonder what he's up to now. Sure enough, he tells me he has recently struck up a friendship with a lady behind the counter in the chemist.

'I only went in for some Lemsip but I didn't want her to think

I was some sort of nancy boy so I slipped a couple of boxes of Durex over the counter with it.'

George is the only person I know who would find buying cold remedies more embarrassing than contraception. They'll have been extra large too. So anyway, he's been calling in there every day. No wonder he offered to get my toothpaste. 'Are you after anything else? Soap?' he asks. He's running out of things to buy.

'She's a recent divorcee. Moved here from Omagh, so she did. She'll be needing a wee bit of a boost,' he says. If I was speaking I'd be sarcastically suggesting he sets up a charity to continue his good work, but for now I'm just listening.

'She asked if Shirley was my wife. I told a wee white lie. Said she was my sister. The lassie'll twig soon enough but sure it's all innocent, Maureen. Only a bit of fun. Shirley lost the bap completely the other day when she saw us chatting. You know what she's like; she can't stand me even speaking to another woman. So our little secret, eh, Maureen?'

No mention of his nineteen-year-old friend who got the Manchester flight on her own.

*

Elizabeth Kelso is here to see me today. Apparently she was in the hospital anyway for a board of trustees meeting. They are trying to raise money for a sensory garden. She's not the sort of person I warm to but she does her bit for the town's charities.

The bell has rung to signify that visiting has ended for the afternoon, but Elizabeth speaks to the Sister and indicates in some way that she outranks her so the rules are bent. Elizabeth is in black and emerald green. She is thinner than me but it doesn't suit her, or do I just want to think that? Her hair is solid as she moves as if made of one piece of plastic, like that on a Lego figure. Her shoes are green suede with gold snaffles. She has a handbag with a clasp that would make a satisfying expensive noise when clicked shut. Elizabeth has poise.

I know I'm not neutral in my views on Elizabeth Kelso, but even the most sympathetic would say she is very conscious of appearances. A dozen or so years back they had a fire in their kitchen. The fire brigade were called. The *Chronicle* referred to it as a chip-pan fire. Elizabeth was mortified. Chip-pan fires belonged in the land of women who nipped out for a packet of fags in their heated rollers, women who wore slacks with stirrups and had husbands who shaved at the kitchen sink.

I remember the conversation outside church the following Sunday. Elizabeth made sure we knew she had been sautée-ing potatoes, not making chips. There was no chip-pan involved. She told the story of the sautéed potatoes so many times; I thought she'd be handing out the recipe.

'Dear Maureen, how are you?' she asks now. She does a patting action in the region of my arm but does not touch me. 'We've been *so* worried.'

Who is 'we', I think. Is it him? Has he talked to her? Does she know he visits?

Elizabeth goes on to talk about the art class. It is herself and the other students who are worried. The class met a couple of times on their own but it wasn't the same without me, she says. I never believe she is being sincere but today she almost sounds it.

'You are an inspiration to us, you know, Maureen. I'm not adventurous or anything. I just want to paint a few cards for Christmas and birthdays. I value the class – I really do.' There is a long pause. 'And I like the "girls" and the chat at coffee.'

I nod encouragingly and say, 'Yes.'

The visitors to the women in the bed opposite wave to me as they leave. Another young woman passes on the way out and shouts, 'Hello, Miss!

'Everyone knows you, Maureen. I still feel I'm a newcomer here, you know. You wouldn't believe it, but it's been hard for me.' She looks pensive and on the way to tears. 'I find it hard to make friends. It comes with the position. Doctor's wife and all that. People see me as a bit... As having... As being somehow different to them. I don't blame them. It's how it's been for years. It's hard to find one's niche in a place like Derryconnor.'

Niche is not a word you would ever associate with Derryconnor.

An auxiliary comes round to replace the water jug. 'How're you doing, Maureen?' Then she smiles shyly at Elizabeth. 'Hello, Mrs Kelso. Do you want to pour a drink for her?'

Elizabeth is hesitant. She was never very hands-on even when her twins were small. She pours the water and hands me my glass.

'I find it hard to get to know people. I know I seem confident but I don't know how to make friends. Never have. Look, I can say it now... You and I never really hit it off and I'm sorry about that. The coldness between us – it's my fault. For a long time I imagined that you and Tom had some sort of liaison. He would come home and say how much he admired you, the terrible time you had when the new baby was abnormal and how hard you worked. He wanted to be your knight in shining armour.

'I watched him watch you for years. You, with your freedom and your outspokenness, your adoring loyal husband. Walter and Tom, the two of them would watch you at events, your hair wild, your face passionate, dancing with Jackie or organising games for the children. I felt you bewitched my Tom. "I'll swing by the McCormacks' to get some water on the way back," he would say. Those boys of mine sat in the car in your yard more times...'

This was her imagination. He hardly came, never came enough. The boys stayed in the car because they were uncomfortable with Jackie who would climb on their knees and ask them for a kiss at an age where they found that all so embarrassing.

'He never lied. He told me where he was. And when he came home I would watch him for signs. I'm an insecure person, you know, Maureen.' She was quiet for a few seconds. 'I would never talk to you like this in normal circumstances. But somehow it's easier when... I used to think you would take him away from me. I know really that you probably never even noticed all of this. You never would have thought the doctor had a thing about you. Senior partner and all that. Happily married. You wouldn't have imagined him being interested in *you*.

'Anyway, it was maybe all in my head at that stage. He denied it. He made me feel that I was being irrational. I begged him not to have you as a patient. Once you were off his list I thought that would be the end of it but I realised there was even more danger when you weren't his patient.'

Now she is shaking and there is an angry nervous flush on her neck and chest.

'When our David started seeing your niece, Claire, I was horrified. She's a lovely girl – not really vet's wife material – but it wasn't that, Maureen. I just couldn't bear any more connection between the two of you. You made my life a misery.'

She makes it sound like a fact rather than an accusation. I am glad of the excuse of aphasia. What would I say to this woman? Did I encourage him? Am I responsible for her unhappiness? If I had had my way she really would have a reason to be angry with me – but she knows of no deeds, only thoughts. I could not be responsible for the thoughts he didn't voice and the intentions he never acted on. *Talk to him and not me.* We look at each other and I can only shake my head. What could I say? That I have suffered too. That it's not true. That I am sorry. She can take her pick of meanings. We sit in silence. I imagine she is trying to work out how to leave with dignity.

We are both relieved when Geraldine from school comes in to see me. Elizabeth says goodbye as if nothing has happened and leaves. Geraldine has been here before, she tells me, but I can remember nothing of the visit, though Shirley showed me a card from the staff as evidence of her visit. Geraldine presses a bag of dried figs into my hands.

'Here, get these down you. I know what hospitals do to your system. Your sister says you are doing much better. Still no speech? We could wheel you into the classroom and you'd still do better than the wee lassie they have doing supply. They're running rings round her.'

She tells me the staffroom gossip. Mostly about inspections, curriculum changes and arguments about lost photocopying.

'I hardly know whether to give you this, Maureen love.' She pulls a thick file from her bag. 'It's from the upper sixth. They put it together for you, but... well, art and tact don't seem to go together. It won't upset you?'

'Yes,' I say, but while shaking my head, and she brings the book round and drags a chair up so she can sit beside me.

'I'm not sure if you can read but this is good. *To the finest art teacher of all time.* Very dramatic, I think they appreciate you better now.'

Geraldine turns the pages and I see what she means. There is a pastiche of *The Scream* with a reasonable representation of my face. A boy called Nick has done an elegant silhouette in red and then dipped one side of it in water so that the ink has run like blood across the page.

'They seemed to treat it as a project. Researching strokes, calling in to see your sister; the whole shebang. I doubt they've put as much effort into any work you've given them. Touching or upsetting?' She looks at me to check. Together we flick through the rest. The ones at the back of the file are more three-dimensional. A girl called Katie has done a relief in chewing gum. I smile. I spent the whole of last year telling her off for chewing gum in class.

'Disgusting, isn't it,' says the fastidious Geraldine. 'She said you'd enjoy it'.

The last piece involves a rope unravelling so that the ends are separated into filaments the breadth of a thread. It has been stiffened and mounted on a black background. It is the one that best symbolises what I feel. Unravelled. I am still for a while and then nod enthusiastically and do a thumbs-up sign so that Geraldine can take a positive message back to the class.

There is more school talk from Geraldine. She tells me she misses me keeping the staffroom light-hearted.

'They're all at each other's throats without you there. And – this is embarrassing but I want to say it. I miss you personally. You being there made work good. I looked forward to Mondays and it's not the same. I hope you get back.' For all her worry about me being upset, it is she who is crying now. Geraldine is a Catholic but married to a Prod, and a couple of the staff made her life tough to start with so I think that's why she took to me.

'I had to tell you, in case...' She doesn't continue.

I hold Geraldine's hand and pat it. I hadn't had time to miss school yet, but now I think about it, I can't bear the thought of not being there for the A-level art exhibition or the leaver's party. I am okay while in here, but the thought that I might never return to my classroom or hang round the kettle at break-time gossiping makes me feel very sad.

'So you liked the book? *Finest art teacher of all time.* You'll have that up on your wall. Anyway, they're a credit to you.'

Geraldine leaves with promises to call in after school once a week and to bring some pictures of the school play.

*

162

I know they will all get fed up visiting if I don't start joining in, but it is hard to imagine a conversation flowing any more. Each word I say either has to be searched for or slips out randomly. So now I try to practise this new speech on Jackie. We've been left alone for a while. Shirley is meeting George in the car park and handing over the keys. They often have transactions like this.

'How's the Centre?' I ask Jackie.

'We did cooking. We had toastie.'

'A toastie?'

'Your throat's better.'

'A wee bit.'

'It was a cheese toastie.'

'Was it... was it... nice?'

'Aye, it was nice.'

Shirley comes back.

'Mummy talks to me,' says Jackie.

'Yes, dear,' says Shirley, and she moves straight on to the subject of the diabolical standard of parking in Derryconnor.

I need not have worried about Jackie giving the game away. I can take refuge in my silence for a little while longer. Jackie strokes my hand and then fiddles with a raw edge on the bed-cover. I'm getting bored in the hospital now. Nothing to do and yet I constantly have a feeling of anticipation, waiting for results, waiting for the drug-round, the night-shift or visiting times.

They leave and I go down into the day room. The news is on very loud. Mo Mowlam, God help her, is still struggling to talk politics with the Ulster men. The Good Friday Agreement is holding but none of us can relax yet. We have been programmed to expect trouble now after nearly three decades of normal days suddenly switching to carnage. I am thinking about the day of the Coleraine bomb.

Mother hated any fuss. There was chaos and activity all around but my mother would not run. It must have been a Monday because it was half-day closing in Derryconnor so Shirley and Claire were there too. There was a booming noise and the whole of Coleraine shuddered. It was at the peak of the bombings round us and often a second explosion would be detonated when people had started to come to. We were well back from the bomb, streets away actually, but you couldn't tell. People were screeching names and running towards the blackness and the noise of buildings crumbling. Jackie was two. I headed for the door but my mother went towards the till with the basket of shopping.

'Mother, come on, we're getting out of here. The whole town could be...'

'I will not be intimidated by these animals. I am paying for my groceries.'

By then the girls at the till were not interested in taking money. Several had run out of the door. One of the shop girls was crying at a phone at the service desk.

'Mammy, I'm all right but there's been a bomb – over near the station. I'm going to see if Declan's okay.'

'We need to go. Come on to the car,' said Shirley in a forced calm voice to my mother.

'Come now, or we're leaving you. I mean it,' I said.

My mother walked at her usual pace while Shirley and I ran to the car and packed away the pushchair and got the children in. The door was open and the engine running when Mother arrived and settled in the car, furious that we'd overruled her.

When we got home, as became routine, we rang the people who knew we'd been to the town to reassure them. We called those we cared about on the off-chance they'd been there. I listened for the name Declan in the list of deaths and casualties, thinking about the wee shop girl on the phone to her mother. We had years of this, hearing the news and wondering if such-and-such was near that bomb. Waiting for names to come up on the next bulletin, and if there was no one you knew, there was a sense of relief but also a sense of shame. Good news for you but not for someone else.

*

On the day of the Good Friday Agreement, I went back to the chapel I had ended up at when I had done the long bleak walk with Jackie in the pram. Like everyone, I couldn't believe the peace would hold. I pulled into the empty car park cautiously. I didn't want to get caught up in one of the services or meet the old priest again so I checked the noticeboard to make sure I could slip in between Easter masses. I saw that now the priest's name was Father Darren McGinlay, a young man's name. The old fella was long gone, I'm sure.

I sat in the dark, polished place and cried with both joy and sorrow; sorrow for all the poor souls who'd died and suffered in this top right-hand corner of Ireland. There was a bit of selfish sorrow for myself too, remembering when I'd last been in that place.

I wonder now why I didn't get more involved in politics and then I could have stood proud with the people who'd worked to get that agreement signed. I went once to a women's peace group meeting. I pretended it was some evening event at school. It's not that Walter would have stopped me or even criticised, it's just that I couldn't face the conversation about something that I wasn't confident about. The meeting was in a community hall and here 'community' doesn't just mean community. It means Catholic community or Protestant community. Th̶i̶s̶ ̶m̶e̶a̶n̶ in a Catholic area and I was nervous. Prejudices I would have laughed at in others surfaced. I locked everything in the boot of the car and even went back to hide the *Belfast Telegraph* under the seat. I wished I had an *Irish News* to leave on view. The Troubles infused everything and made even the most reasonable people cautious and superstitious.

The women at the meeting were lovely but the main group were all called things like Soirse and Siobhan and Grainne – names I couldn't have spelled. There were a couple of Quakers too; calm, still women contrasting with the Roman Catholic girls who were swearing and smoking and telling their stories like at an Alcoholics Anonymous meeting. I said little. What would I have said? 'I'm Maureen and I'm a Protestant and nothing terrible has happened to me. I've lost no one through these Troubles and I have no sons to stop joining paramilitary organisations. I'm just pig sick of this place and all the petty sectarian nonsense and the fact we can't be proud of anything as Protestants. We're the white South Africans of the country, but I've never done anything wrong. I've never discriminated, nor fought, nor hated.'

Anyway I stayed at the meeting and signed a petition, drew a slightly skew-whiff dove on a poster and helped draft a leaflet to be handed out at some peace event that in the end I never went to. There was a nun at the meeting who winced at some of the language and 'Sorry, Sister' punctuated the evening's discussion.

She asked if they wanted a prayer at the end and the main woman said, 'Nah, you're all right there, Sister. I'm sure we'll all pray to our gods and goddesses later.' This time she said 'Sister' as if it was a sisterhood thing rather than a religious title.

As I got into the car after the meeting, I saw one of the older women at the bus stop. One of her sons had been killed. She pronounced killed, 'kilt' and contracted each word so phrases were like the rounds of automatic fire that had taken her son. I pulled over and offered to run her home.

'That'd be great, darlin'.'

In the car we chatted about weather and gardens. I apologised for the smell in the car and said it was a real farmer's car.

'I've never met a farmer,' she said. 'I work in the shirt factory.'

I'd never met anyone who worked in a factory. We were from two different worlds. We were silent for a while.

'Do you think there'll be peace in our lifetime?' I asked her.

'God only knows. Not if men are in charge. Us women are used to sorting out fights between boys.'

We laughed. And in the end she was right. It was a woman who finally got the thing signed. Mo Mowlam got agreement between men who could hardly even say good morning to each other. She'd walked around Stormont in her bare feet, wig off, swearing and all but knocking the boys' heads together to get there.

As we got near the estate where she lived, the woman told me to drop her off at the bus stop.

'Sure I'll take you to the door,' I said. 'It's no bother.'

'Augh, this is grand here. Don't want any questions,' she said. 'You know what they're like.'

I wondered who 'they' were. I hoped the Troubles were over for her.

18

Elizabeth Kelso is here to see me again today. I am feeling good. Ready for home. The headaches are gone and I am much less tired. I won't be able to tell until I am in the house how bad I really am.

Elizabeth has brought some pretty soap.

'Dear only knows what the hospital soap does to your skin if you're in here for a while, I'll put it in your locker. Look, I'm sorry I got into a bit of a state last time. You're in hospital and you're still very ill and I shouldn't... Well, I'm sorry. '

He hasn't told her I'll be going home soon. She settles down and talks for a while about the boys and how great they are and then: 'So Tom has been in to see you?'

I am worried this is a trick question so I smile and for once don't say yes automatically.

'I know he's been down most days.' She looks ahead rather than at me. 'He's a very committed GP, a very good man. Well, I should know, I've been married to him for thirty-two years.'

Elizabeth Kelso has a determined look on her face today.

The Minister comes in, still wearing his bicycle clips and fluorescent waistcoat, over-snug on top of his sports jacket.

'Mrs Kelso – and how are you doing?'

'Oh I'm grand, and yourself?'

He points to his unusually bright get-up. 'You'll have to report back to the doctor that I'm doing more exercise.' He turns to me. 'And Maureen. Home tomorrow, isn't that great?'

'She's going home?' Ellizabeth's voice is sharp and she looks at me as if I've been concealing information.

'Oh yes, so I'm told,' says Rev Purdie, fumbling with the clip of his cycle helmet. He has an apologetic tone although he looks uncertain of what he has done wrong.

Elizabeth leaves a little abruptly and I am left to listen to the Minister talk about God and the 'good news' and then the real, not so good news – and finally, an indiscreet murmured rhetorical question.

'Mrs Kelso. Not the easiest person to read, is she? I don't know what I've done to her. Never mind, Maureen. There's a good day coming.'

Tanya rattles along the corridor with a sealed plastic bag full of tablets for me and a letter for my GP. She expresses surprise that my GP isn't Tom Kelso as he's been calling in so often. Reverend Purdie backs away, wishing me luck and threatening to cycle the whole way out to the farm. It's really going to happen. I'm going home. It's what I want, but I'm scared.

*

The speech therapist comes to the ward to say goodbye and gives me an out-patient appointment and a leaflet about a club for stroke victims. I am glad there is no one here to listen to our conversation.

'Well, last day,' she says. I think she wants to give me a hug.

'Yes. Thanks be to God,' I say. I don't know where that came from. I meant to say thank you.

Mandy smiles. 'How are you feeling about going home?'
'Okay.'
'Just okay? You have to start speaking to them.'
'Yes.'
'By rights I should be referring you to a psychologist.'
'Yes, yes, okay.'
'Do you talk to *any* of them?'
'Yes – Jackie.'

'Well, that's good. It will build your confidence up.'

She sounds relieved. She doesn't remember who Jackie is and why she is the one to whom I can speak. I will talk soon, but there is more listening to do first.

19

We pull into the yard. Claire is out of the car and round to open the passenger door with the speed of one of the Special Services fellas who used to shadow Paisley. I walk into my home, uncertain whether I'll ever be able to leave it again. The kitchen is disinfected to Shirley's standards which would shame most operating theatres. I pause while she displays the contents of the fridge and freezer. I will not starve anyway. There is a basket of letters and cards on the kitchen table.

'I opened the ones that looked like bills. The rest were mostly circulars or cards. I did bring some of them to the hospital but anyway you can go through that lot at your leisure. Claire, take them through to the other room.'

In the living room there is the faint burning smell of dust on electric heaters turned on for the first time in autumn. A new blanket lies over the back of an old person's chair. The chair is for me. Shirley guides me to it and I sit down heavily. My heavy heart manifested physically. What now?

Shirley comes in with a cup of tea. Jackie will be dropped back soon. They hadn't told her that I was coming home in case there was some problem. I begin to worry that she will be confused and anxious if she is dropped back here instead of Shirley's after all this time but it's too late now. We sit confined in a room rarely used for a casual cup of tea, my sister and I. There is an edgy silence as if we have only just got away with something. A new picture hangs above the fireplace, a dark heathery-coloured landscape. A picture I don't recall buying or hanging. I gesticulate towards it.

'Yes, I like it,' says Shirley. 'It looks well there. When did you get it?'

I shrug.

'Did you do it?' asks Shirley.

I shake my head – but it is like the sort of picture I paint.

Shirley starts trying to piece together my last stroke-free hours like Hercule Poirot. I cannot remember the weeks before the stroke but she doesn't know that, so focuses instead on the immediate run-up. I was not at work. I had left home after 8.30, as apparently I had waved Jackie off in the morning. At exactly 10.09 I had picked up a ticket in the car park. The passers-by had made the 999 call at 10.12. God, my parking must have been better than normal that day. Shirley had found the parking ticket when they had gone to pick up the car.

'Any phone messages for Aunt Maureen?' asks Claire.

'A few. The optician called and several people rang, but by the time I listened to the messages, the news had got around and there was no need to call them back. And there was a wrong number – well, several. From a Scottish woman desperate to get hold of some fella that stood her up. That filled the machine up so I deleted them all, but no more in the last week or two. They all knew you were in hospital. You know what this place is like.'

Claire helps me with the sorting. She uses the paper-knife to slit open the letters. It's something she and Jackie have always liked doing. They used to call the paper-knife 'the little sword'. She opens several charity requests, an adult education newsletter and my union fees bill. Reading is still a struggle. She reads the longer messages on cards aloud, sometimes doing impersonations if she knows the sender. The next letter is in a buff envelope, but the address is handwritten.

'Oh, a letter from Scotland.' She starts to read in a stage Scottish lilt, but that doesn't last long...

*

Dear Maureen,

What happened? I was there. I checked a hundred times I was in the right place. Is everything okay? Did you get cold feet?

I know it's been a long time. Thirty-five years. That's why I sent the text about the red coat; otherwise, we could have been sitting in the same hotel bar and not recognised each other. But why didn't you come, Mo, and why ignore my calls and texts? I would understand. I'm half furious and half really worried. All these years we've sent the Christmas letter. I know about the school and the farm and Jackie. You know about the shops and the grandchildren. But we've never talked about how we came to be together. I understood why you wanted to keep it secret and 'never go there again' as they say. Is that why you didn't turn up?

I waited for three hours. Four cappuccinos. But I went back the next day. Remember, we had dithered about whether to make it Friday or Saturday and I thought I'd got it wrong.

So why didn't you come? We had three months together. In the same room. We went through so much. I was so scared and you held my hand, matching the pressure as if you could feel the pain that I did. And when they took me to the clinic and you stood crying and we thought we'd never see each other again. God knows how I got them to let me back in again, that night I brought the wee bottle of Bells. Mo, don't cut me off. I, of all the people in the whole world, know how you were that night. I thought you would die of crying. I'm crying now because I worry that I have brought this all up for you again.

Agnes

*

Claire is uncertain what to do next. She knows that this is something I would not have chosen for her to find out about, but she also knows it is easier for me that it is her and not her mother who has opened the letter.

'Is it... what? I don't know what to do. She hasn't got it wrong? It is for you, isn't it?'

I put my hand on my chest and nod.

'Should I ring her? Her number's on your phone if she texted you.' She reaches into my bag. The phone's been off for weeks, months maybe. She presses the on key. 'Twenty-seven missed calls.'

Claire and I sit silent. She dials to get voice messages. I hear the beginnings of one.

'Mo, where are you? Am I in the right place?'

Claire listens to the very end of the message, then presses a button and puts the phone down. It keeps pinging with messages on her lap. Every so often there is a small intake of breath and she turns to me but it doesn't come to anything. Then finally, she says, 'I have to ring her, all these calls. She's worried. Can I ring her?'

Claire looks at me and I nod again.

'Okay. We'll wait until Mum's out of the way.'

Claire remembers what she is supposed to be doing and she lifts the silver paper-knife and opens the next letter. Each letter is unfolded and passed to me and I point to the bin and say, 'Bin,' but any more complicated instructions have to be chosen from a list of options provided by Claire. We are both disturbed by the letter.

I didn't remember being in touch with Agnes, let alone organising to see her. What else is missing? What other facts or feelings have been blocked? Claire lifts the letter from Agnes and folds it and puts it in her jeans pocket. Her jeans are so tight I can see the outline of the paper through the denim. She shows me Agnes's home and mobile number stored in my phone. I have entered them. It must be true.

'I'll phone her later,' she promises. 'Maybe I should tell her not to tell me anything – or should I?'

Claire is desperate to know. She's hoping Agnes is a talker but Agnes won't talk. I know she won't.

What am I going to do about Agnes? She needs to know what has happened, but does Claire need to know everything? I can sense my niece trying to suck information out of me just by looking at me. But at least she'll understand my reticence as far as her mother getting to know. On the other hand, does it matter any more?

Shirley is heading to the shop, satisfied that I am safe. The door shuts. We hear the car leave the yard.

'Shall I call this Agnes woman?'

I nod. Claire makes a cup of tea first. She has caught this habit from her mum and her grandmother before her. Now settled, she starts to dial. I somehow didn't think that she'd ring from the same room as me. I don't know if I want to hear what she says.

'Hello, is that Agnes? Oh... is she available? My name is Claire McNair. I'm a friend of Maureen's.'

There is a pause and Claire looks at me and smiles reassuringly.

'Hello, you don't know me. I'm Maureen McCormack's niece. Yes, that's right – I'm Claire.' Claire looks at me, surprised that this stranger is familiar with our family tree. 'My aunt wanted me to call you. She's not been well and she missed meeting you... Pardon? Please will you say that again?'

I imagine Claire is foxed by Agnes's strong Aberdonian accent or that Agnes is upset.

'No. Well, yes it was serious, but she's doing better. She's had a wee stroke. No. She's here now. Her speech is affected, but she's well enough.'

I overhear Agnes down the line say, 'Can you let me talk to her?'

'She can only listen,' says Claire. She looks at me, then points to the phone, her face questioning.

'Yes,' I say. I reach my hand out for the phone and wave her out of the room.

Agnes's voice is still young. Maybe it's dropped in pitch a little since our youth, but if you didn't know, you could believe she was still sixteen

'Maureen, is that you?'

'Yes.'

'Can I talk? Is it okay?'

'It's okay.'

'I'm sorry about the messages. I was worried, not cross with you. Well, a bit cross. Affronted. What did I say? It might have come over all wrong.'

'It's okay.'

'I couldn't understand why you would be all keen and then not turn up or answer your mobile. I've been that worried. I never thought about you not being well. I still think of you as a wee lassie, of course.

I've been nearly ready to go to the doctor to get tablets I've felt so low about it. You and me, we go back a long way. Isn't that right?'

'Yes.'

'Can I come and see you? Are you doing okay now?'

'Yes.'

'And Claire? Is she looking after you? And is Jackie all right and all?'

'Jackie. She's okay.'

'I thought you'd taken umbrage over something I'd said, or that you didn't want to remember back to that time.'

'It's okay.'

'And is it just your speech? Can you get about?'

'Mmm. It's okay.'

'Can I ask Claire? Can Claire tell me the whole story?'

'Yes.'

'And can I phone you again? And come over?'

'Yes. Yes.'

'Get Claire on for me then. And I won't say anything about anything. I said stuff in the letter. I wouldn't have...'

'It's okay.'

'Get Claire then.'

They have rigged up a wee bell for me. I ring it and Claire comes in almost at once and I hand the phone to her.

Claire tells Agnes the story of what happened and some of it is news to me. I don't know if she's embellishing it for dramatic effect, but her talk of mercy dashes and heroic passers-by breaking the passenger window of my car and getting me into the recovery position is faintly embarrassing.

'At least now we know where she was headed the day she had the stroke – yes, that actual day.... No, no, not at all, it would have happened anyway. It was actually good luck in a way, as she was nearer the hospital... No, it was no bother. Well, ring any time. No – actually text me first to check.'

Claire gives her mobile number and hands the phone to me to say farewell. I manage to say goodbye to Agnes, then begin to cry. I'm still delicate. Still shaky. Claire pats me.

'She sounds nice. Very Scottish though.' She says it as if they are usually mutually exclusive. 'You know her from a long time ago?'

'Yes,' I say. I mean to sound neutral but it comes out plaintive and brings on the crying again. I hear an engine in the yard and recognise the sound of the mini-bus that brings Jackie back from the Centre.

'Yes, yes.' I point towards the back door. I want to make sure that Claire is there to reassure Jackie. Claire twigs and runs to greet her. I am still unsure about the timescale of my period in hospital. Will a return home be unsettling for my daughter?

I hear Claire talking (drama school projection) but can't catch Jackie's voice as the cousins walk through the house.

'Yes, it is a surprise and there is someone you will be very pleased to see sitting in the front room. No, not him – someone you know already.'

Jackie comes in. Sees me, says: 'It's only Mummy.'

Claire laughs. 'I hope you're not easily offended, Auntie Maureen. She thought it might be Terry Wogan.'

It feels strange being here and being inactive, as if I am a ghost. They talk to me but I am mostly watching.

*

My first meal at home from the hospital is spaghetti. Claire has followed an authentic Italian recipe for the sauce but the tomatoes round here have seen little sun and she is disappointed with the flavour. She squeezes a bit of tomato ketchup into the saucepan and stirs it round. Claire has not thought through the choice of pasta. I'm still uncoordinated and my so-called bad arm is a little like one of those grabbing fairground machines reaching for a furry toy. Jackie always found spaghetti tricky and she methodically severs each piece into tiny lengths and uses her pudding spoon to eat it. Claire is upset. She wanted to get everything right for my first night home and had prepared it as carefully as she would for a date, a bit like I was when I first married Walter. It tastes fine to me.

'Yes, yes,' I say in protest to her self-criticism and give it the thumbs-up.

'It's nice,' says Jackie when asked.

The girls, as I think of them, though Jackie is twenty-six and Claire twenty-nine, begin clearing up the kitchen. Claire has exhausted herself with the effort of cooking and moans about the lack of a dishwasher. I walk into the front room to escape the clatter and the sound of the news on Radio Ulster. Jackie soon tires of the housework and wanders in to see me. I decide I need to get to bed even though it's barely 8.30 pm.

'I'm old,' I say to Jackie as I edge forward on the chair to get up as the occupational therapist taught me.

'Not as old as the Queen,' says Jackie.

'Yes,' I say, 'the Queen of Hearts.'

'She died.'

'The Queen died?'

'No, Princess Di.'

I know Princess Diana died but it feels like a film I watched, rather than news. It was last year, I think, but it feels more recent, as if some of the time in between has concertinaed. Some things in the run-up to the stroke are there tucked away somewhere, recognisable and retrievable. Other things, even when Shirley goes over them slightly impatiently, are not. Wiped forever, perhaps? It's like when my mother kept calling me Helen in the last weeks of her life as if she had forgotten my entire existence and slotted me into the place of her sister.

Up in the bedroom, Claire and Jackie wrestle with the mattress. Shirley had left it leaning against the radiator to air it. It is hard watching the two of them struggle and not being able to help. Claire gets the bed-linen from the hot press and I make an unsuccessful attempt at putting a pillow in a pillowcase while she and Jackie make up the bed. The bed is raised on blocks and there is a device for me to grab, fitted above where my head will be. Although I am slow, I manage to get ready for bed myself. Claire is lurking outside like a sales assistant in a posh dress shop.

'Yes,' I call.

She comes in.

'Brilliant, you hardly need me.' She is relieved that her offer to stay with me is going to involve less personal care than she thought. It is early – a quarter to nine – but I am very tired. The bell has come up with me and Claire tells me I can ring it any time. It's a strange relief when she leaves the room and pulls the door to.

20

I got home two days ago. Yesterday there was an influx of visitors, made up of those fearful of hospitals or scared of what they might find when they got there. Neighbours, happy to call in with a paper or a tin of tray bakes and to take a wee cup of tea, but not sure enough of their status to become hospital visitors. So we have been busy.

Today we ended up with two copies of the *Derryconnor Times*. Claire and I read it page by page together with her asking questions about whom, what or where. My speech is still very limited but I now communicate a bit more. Claire folds the paper so I have a manageable section to hold. I can't concentrate on the reading so I look at the pictures and the headlines and the occasional article if she draws my attention to it. They are planning to close the casualty department at Derryconnor Hospital. We all know it makes financial sense, but important people are protesting, estimating how long the journey will take to the nearest alternative. Claire laughs at the notion that Derryconnor has a 'rush hour' which the paper says will make journey times unacceptable. Tom Kelso is concerned, the Mayor is alarmed and the head of the ambulance service is not allowed to comment.

'So, if things had been different, would you two have got together?'

She does not mention his name but we both have our papers open at the article which covers the whole half-page.

'Umm?' I say, looking at her quizzically.

'You know who I mean. Everybody saw it. Even the twins used to joke about it. They didn't think that anything would happen, but they could tell he had a thing about you – like Jackie and Terry Wogan. Mrs Kelso would hardly have your name mentioned in the house, apparently. There was a big row once – but you know what she's like. A complete control freak.'

I didn't like the idea of everyone making a joke about this or of Elizabeth being upset.

Claire picks up my reaction and looks at me, concerned.

'Don't worry about it. I shouldn't have mentioned it. You being quiet makes me talk even more.'

*

Claire is clumsy in the kitchen, clanging about, opening cupboard after cupboard, poking around searching for stuff, hissing 'shit' when she lifts something hot. The sounds of her kitchen, I suspect, are of a fork piercing tight cellophane twice, a hum and then a ping. I envy her generation. There is no guilt about ready meals.

Claire tells me she wants to learn to cook while she is here. It may be true, though to start with I thought it was set up as a therapy for me. Well, if she thinks that, she's wrong. If I could speak I'd joke that I'll need therapy *afterwards* as it's torture to watch her at times. She peels potatoes as if restoring a Faberge egg. When she cooks she has the pan on high and I can see the oil japping all over the stove, newly cleaned by Shirley. Every pot and pan in the kitchen is used. By the time the meal is over, Claire is exhausted. But she does talk while she cooks and so it is company. She is lively. She is uplifting to be with. When Jackie is there they work together. Jackie is the washer-upper.

'You need to get a dishwasher,' Jackie says, copying her cousin, but she is happier being kept busy, doing things for Claire that she would never do for me. When people call, Jackie tells them that she is looking after me until my leg and throat get better. Sometimes she stops halfway through the dishes and runs over to hug me, rubbing her warm wet hands on my back. I can tell she's missed me. This is perfect for her – attention from Claire, and me here sitting still and not being able to tell her off.

'I'm having a biscuit,' she sometimes says when Claire's not around, and helps herself. 'Do you want a biscuit, Mum?' Funnily enough she doesn't overdo the biscuit-eating; knowing she can seems to be enough. Why did we have all those battles in the past, I wonder. I am learning so much, now that I have time to look, learning about myself.

'You like having Claire here?' I start a conversation with Jackie that may not go anywhere.

'Aye, Claire's nice.'

'Yes.' I smile in agreement.

'When will Jim come for his tea?'

Claire calls over, 'Don't worry, Jackie, Jim has tea at his own house.'

Jackie sits beside me and I reach round with my good arm and hug her as tight as I can.

'Love you, my mum.' Jackie rests her cheek against mine. 'I'm being good, aren't I?'

'Yes, very good.'

I am pleased she can use the word 'love' more freely than her father. I remember asking Walter one day, 'Do you love me? You never say you do.'

He just said, 'Sure, I wouldn't have married you if I hadn't loved you, would I?'

That was the best he could do.

*

Our evening meals are like dinner parties. Claire lights candles she has brought back from the shop and there is a great fuss about serviette-folding. It takes me back to the days when Shirley and I used to play house. If I was my normal self, I'd get more bored, but I'm still repairing. I need easy thoughts after the stroke, like you need bland food after an operation. I have felt anger though, in this past week. I feel angry with Walter again. I see how Jackie thrives on love and attention and how, if she'd had that properly from two people, she might have done better. But there again, it wouldn't have taken away the Down's.

When the table-setting ritual is finished, there is a whispered conversation and Jackie comes over and tells me, 'Dinner is served, madam.'

Of course, I know that, because I am sitting there right by the stove – but it is part of their fun. I can get up and over to the table fairly easily now. I am still not what you'd call nimble but it's okay. I am hampered by the fact that the seat is slippery. Claire has insisted on putting a 'throw', as she calls it, over the chair the OT brought. We are all hungry and we eat silently. I think of other, busy times in this kitchen.

*

Shirley and I were around seven and eight. It must have been autumn. A weekend. Mother was making marmalade and we were helping. The marmalade wouldn't set and my mother was hot and cross, standing guard over the preserving pan. There was a story of a little girl who had been scalded in an accident involving hot jam, recounted each time the preserving pan came out. The story, combined with a hot sticky kitchen environment, always made me feel sick. It was part of a series of stories we heard many times from my mother, like one about the girl whose eye was put out by the garden cane, the child who ran with a lolly in their mouth and the boy who threw keys and scarred his wee sister. Life with Mother was full of stories about terrible things that might happen.

Every ten minutes she spooned marmalade on to a cold saucer and I would be sent to the fridge with it. A little time would pass and I would get the saucer out and Mother would pull her finger over the surface to check if it was going to set and then tut grumpily when it didn't. The marmalade was then scraped back into the preserving pan and I had to wash the saucer, and then the ritual was repeated. Eventually the saucer of marmalade was perfect – the surface rucked up like the skin on the back of my grandmother's hand.

We were all hungry and tired from washing jam jars and turning the handle on the machine that minced up the orange skin. When the jars had all been filled with marmalade, Mother got the jam-cover kit out and dipped the cellophane into hot water and fastened it with an elastic band so it was stretched as tight as a Lambeg drum. When she got to the last jar, it skidded out of her hand and smashed onto the hard terrazzo floor. Her apron and legs were splattered with hot marmalade and she said, 'Damn!' loudly and angrily. We had never heard her say a bad word before.

Shirley was washing sticky spoons and ladles at the sink wearing an apron that was too long for her. I was busy writing the labels for the jam jars in fancy lettering and drawing a tiny picture of an orange in colouring pencils on each one.

'Are you not finished the labels? For pity's sake, Maureen, get on with it. You don't have to make a whole circus out of it. Your father'll be in for his tea and there's not a thing ready.'

My father was so laid-back he'd have been happy with marmalade sandwiches if it would have kept her calm, but my mother's regime was important to her. She ripped the labels out of my hand and passed me the brush and shovel to clear up the flowing glass and marmalade mix on the floor. I did my best but she told me I was making it worse. Father came in as if he had sensed the tension even from outside.

'Here, Maureen, I'll clear that up, I'm dirty anyway. And then I have a fancy for cheese on toast tonight and I don't trust you girls to get it right.'

My father's only contribution to the culinary life in Ballinstavey was cheese on toast – half a soda farl bubbling with yellow cheddar – and at the table he would swirl each person's initial with brown sauce on their slice. On the cheese-on-toast evenings, Mother was made to sit down. There was a calm in the house. My mother would warn us against burning the roof of our mouths and we would all congratulate Dad on his great recipe.

This space by the stove in this kitchen was where my grandmother sat. She used to talk to me while she cleaned the eggs with glass paper. I was not trusted to touch the eggs but I would be sitting by her, shelling peas or doing another task where I couldn't go wrong. I never remember talking unless we both had a job to do. My grandmother was very upright and tall for a woman of that generation, but if she were to appear now and walk among Claire's friends she would be only a little above average height. She was stout but not fat. She wore corsetry and clothing that looked as if it was sewn to her like a well-made button-back chair.

Grandma was strong even when I first remember her and could carry a calf under one arm and a bucket in the other hand. Her legs were always bare above her wellingtons, except on Sundays or when visiting, when she would wear stockings held up in a twist above the knee. She would put a thru'penny bit in the top of her stocking, twist it and tuck it into the top. The arrangement seemed effective. She was not the sort of woman who would have mishaps with hosiery. She sounds formidable but she was less frightening than my mother. Perhaps grandmothers always are? They have had time to mellow. She would always tell my mother to stop fussing. When visiting people's houses she would say, 'I'll just have a cup of tea in my hand,' meaning that she did not want side-plates, doilies or trolleys and nests of tables pulled out.

She didn't trust machinery and had a big fear of farm accidents. If my father started the tractor she would pull everyone back against a wall. On drives in the car she held on to a strap hanging above the door and the other hand gripped me hard. I would sometimes have to tell her she was hurting me. There were pictures of her as a young girl wearing a long dress and pinafore. I told her she was 'historical'. She laughed and told me it was better than being hysterical.

I haven't thought about those days for years. It's as if I am watching repeats of old TV shows, now that I've finally got the time to switch them on.

21

Tom Kelso's first visit when I am back in Balinstavey is stilted. Claire doesn't know whether to go or stay. With other visitors she makes tea and helps fill in the gaps in the conversation. She is a novelty so they mostly talk to her about what it's like to be on the TV. Tom has already chatted to her and there is still vague embarrassment over the fact that she was once going to be his daughter-in-law.

'So, will I put the kettle on, Dr Kelso?'

'I'm okay now, Claire.'

She sits for a few minutes and then, 'I'll go now and sort out stuff in the kitchen.'

When she leaves, Tom moves closer to me. I don't think we have ever been in this room together alone.

'How are you doing? Are you keeping well?'

'Yes.'

'Bored?'

'Yes.' I smile at him. No one else has even thought of that.

'You don't fancy painting or something?'

I screw up my nose.

'The waiting room could do with a lick of paint'.

I smile at his attempt at a joke.

'You don't need a prescription or anything?'

I shake my head.

He changes tone so suddenly that I flinch.

'Augh, Maureen, why did I waste my whole bloody life? Two weeks in Malta every year, making meaningless conversation. Christmas or New Year in Dublin with Elizabeth's family and in between working all the hours God sends. Two sons who phone once a fortnight to get interrogated by their mother. No point, that's what I think now. I'm fed up with the whole shooting match.'

He looks really miserable, as if he's suddenly realised his own age. It's all about how *he* feels.

Claire turns the door handle and then turns it again before she actually opens the door.

'You don't need anything, Aunt Maureen?'

'Yes,' I say. I can't say no yet but she has now worked out which yeses are real.

'We were thinking about going out for a walk. Yes, Maureen, a bit of fresh air?' says Tom.

He helps me into my coat and Claire accessorises me with her scarf and hat and reaches for the aluminium walking stick.

'If she hangs on to me, can she manage?' asks Tom.

'I think so,' says Claire.

So he and I walk arm-in-arm, the way I dreamed about. He puts his hand on top of mine, I stand taller than before, trying not to lean so it seems less like he's helping me. Outside, we look towards the hills and he sighs again.

'Elizabeth's driving me mad. Menopause or something. Everything I do is wrong – even coming to see you. Oh, I don't know. It's all so... It's such a bloody waste.'

He never moans about Elizabeth and I never moaned about Walter. We kept our conversations free of any mention of them. I don't like this.

We can't go far. We walk down to the lane that leads to the bungalow and look across the low fields. He is holding me tight, terrified I'll fall. He sighs and his voice changes as if he knows that I need a change to this mood. He talks about the twins, though it is clear that they have their own lives and he feels distant from them. He works hard and worries about his patients, but of course he can't talk about them. There is silence. I realise that of the two of us, I am the talker. He turns me and pulls me to him. For a hug. A comforting hug. It's me who's comforting him.

We return to the house and Claire is pacing with the cordless phone.

Shirley doesn't quite trust Claire to look after me. At least once a day she calls from her mobile and I can hear Claire's frustration.

'No, nothing. Oh, okay, bring bread – nothing else.'

While she's on the phone, Tom helps me off with my coat, whispers that he's going. He puts his hands on my shoulders and kisses my forehead.

Claire sits down, tired with exasperation but soon forgets about it.

'I spoke to you in the hospital about this boyfriend of mine. I don't know if you remember me telling you?' she asks.

'Yes'. I nod vigorously. I want her to know I remember most things, but on the other hand I wouldn't know what I didn't remember.

'I've been thinking a lot about him. We talk on the phone. He's still keen. He understands about me being here – he thinks I'm some sort of saint actually. He wants to come over to see me, for a long weekend. This weekend as a matter of fact. I haven't told Mum and Dad anything. Would it be all right?'

'Yes.'

'Is that a real yes or a stroke yes?'

'*Yes,*' I say very emphatically, and smile. 'At least *you* won't be able to interrogate him, but Mum... and Dad, I can't imagine what they'll be like. It's probably a good thing, my being here, it might help me make up my mind. Absence makes the heart grow fonder and all that.'

So the boyfriend is coming this weekend. I don't think she's even told me his name. She's going to have to tell Shirley.

Shirley, the woman who wants to know everything first, is the one who is told last.

Tom's visit has left me feeling cross again. My moods are unpredictable. Perhaps they always have been but I've not had the time to sit with them and work out why. He is so much part of my life but we have never walked arm-in-arm before. Never walked down to look at that view. Never run out of things to say.

When Shirley and I were wee, that lane seemed a long way from the house. Another land. We were real country girls, even though when I got older I didn't really like to think of myself like that. I thought my natural home would be Paris or New York. Back then, we were always outside. Always grubby and a bit damp. We had special places, made hideouts and started collections.

In the middle of one of the fields was a fairy thorn. We would go there to get out of the house. Round the thorn bush there was our accumulation of stones and horseshoes, bits of old clay smoking pipes and snail shells. Shirley and I used to sit there making necklaces. We would thread rosehips and haws and some little berries that looked like polystyrene that we called snow-bobbles. We would make salads from leaves that we called tartys and chives from the garden and eat them off big sycamore leaves. We knew every patch of nettles and the nearest corresponding clump of dock leaves. The bush gave a bit of shelter from the rain and there was an old bit of wood tucked under that we would take out to sit on. One day we couldn't both sit on it. We had grown too big.

I never thought to walk across those fields any more. Never had time to appreciate old rusty bedsteads placed in hedges years ago by Dad to keep the sheep in; now incorporated into the hedge by ivy. Will I ever be able to hop over the gate at the end of the lane and travel by stepping stone across the burn towards the bungalow to see Jim?

I look out of the window towards what Shirley and I called 'the ghost trees', a line of silver birch standing out in the gloom of the late afternoon among the low dark bushes at the end of the field.

Again I question my preoccupation over the years. Tom Kelso: when would I see him? What did he feel? Would he remember Jackie's birthday? Would he call up with my mother's prescription? Would he be elected to the school governors? What a lot of time and energy I put into all that. When he talks of Elizabeth, I wonder was Shirley right? Would it have been less harmful to have an affair and let it burn itself out, instead of all this fantasy and angst? Elizabeth hasn't been protected anyway. Claire says everyone knew. I feel embarrassed.

I wonder what things would really have been like with Tom Kelso. The night of the party, our lovemaking was not gentle or thoughtful. What sort of lover would he have been? Would he have been like Jim, who lowered me on to the bed, parted my legs and seemed to worship me with his mouth, his hands gentle against the trembling tendons at the top of my thighs. Was the fun and easiness with Jim really unusual? Maybe Tom Kelso would have been buttoned up and unimaginative – not like my fantasy at all. I had years to develop my dream version of him, but perhaps Walter was really the norm. How will I ever know now... ?

I have been drifting but now I remember something: Jim knew why I'd gone to Belfast. Why had I told him and no one else? Trying to remember feels like watching a film you've seen before but you just can't recall how it ends.

22

A letter arrived from Agnes this morning. She must have started writing it the moment she put the phone down. An envelope within an envelope. The inner envelope said *For your eyes only*. It reminded me of how much fun she'd been, and how eloquent a storyteller at the Green Grove.

*

Claire seems a nice lassie. I forget she's grown up. It's funny how you think other people's lives stand still even though your own life races ahead. I know I'm old now. I am on HRT but in an effort to keep my ageing secret from my husband I hide the pills in my handbag. I nearly ate one of my mother's spare hearing aid batteries when I tried to sneakily take my pill without putting my glasses on. Vanity, it's a terrible thing. I've always been conscious that because I had Rory so young, people would be thinking I'm older than I am.

*

She talks about the chain of shops and bizarre new sausages with apricots or prunes, spiced with paprika or tarragon. She writes about Andy with such love and delight, even though it's thirty-four years since they were almost separated by her parents when she was sent to the Green Grove Home.

*

Andy is worried he is getting fat so we have long walks every weekend. Even the dog dreads it but it's been good for us. We still hold hands and talk as if we were court-ing. He is not putting on weight at all. He's about right now. He was always a skinny malinky. I used to make him wear thermals under his suit when we went out, to bulk him up a bit so people wouldn't think I was starving him.

It must have been hard, being on your own these past few years. I'd thought of coming over before, you know. It's easier to explain things like how we know each other as time goes on. You know, I remember that time in Green Grove with fondness. I never had a sister but that place was full of something like sisterly love. I'm sure you see it differently – a time of loss more than anything positive. That's why I worried that you backed out of the meeting.

*

In fact, I too looked back on that time fondly. Agnes was the only girl I still kept in touch with, but I remembered them all as if I had a class photo all labelled up. Big Fiona and wee Fiona, Jeanette, Adele, Wilma, Rhona, Maggie and the red-haired girl whose story was too terrible to tell. She was so shy she'd hardly tell us her name so we called her 'Ginger Nut' which seems cruel but she was so hungry for affection she was thrilled to get a nick-name.

*

Boffy, Claire's man, has arrived. He is nervous but eager to come across as easy-going. Boffy looks out of the window a lot. At first

I thought he was bored but I realise that it is so long since a stranger visited that I have forgotten that the view across the hills is beautiful. He seems almost blinded by the greenness of it all. He has been in London too long. The sun is shining today so he hasn't worked out that the secret of our green grass here is that it hardly ever stops raining. He's a boy who needs some colour in his life. I say boy but he must be pushing thirty. He needs someone like Claire – but does she need someone like him? I will wait and see.

'Have you always lived here?'

'Yes,' I say and mime a baby in this bizarre new made-up sign language that I presume everyone will understand.

'You were born here?'

I nod.

'Wow.'

I can see him thinking, Oh God, I said 'wow'. I must sound stupid. He doesn't want to get anything wrong in front of Claire's family.

'I was born in London and I've never moved. Now I've got a job in Edinburgh – it'll be a real culture shock.'

'Yes,' I say, though I don't really agree. All cities are the same. Coming here is the culture shock.

'I can see how Claire likes returning back here.'

'Yes.' Though again I am not sure. Claire has been ambivalent about coming back for a while and I am surprised she has lasted so long this time. At that moment, my niece comes in.

'Fancy a walk, Boffy?'

Of course he is up like a shot, keen to be alone with her. The last thing he wants is to be stuck inside, making conversation with me.

I can see them through the window. He is wearing an old bobble hat of Jackie's. Claire has wrapped this man up warm. I can tell she likes him. Her hand is slipped in his pocket. She never stops talking and he listens. His eyes leave her only to look at what she is showing him. I can't believe there is that much to say about our farm. There is so much expression in her face that I can almost follow what she is saying. She is pointing out the boundary of our land. My land. He probably thinks I am rich but doesn't realise that a lot of it is too boggy to work or graze, and the rest is let out for a pittance because I am no business-woman. The dog snaps round his heels but he handles it well. He is not going to let Claire think he is scared.

When they come into the back porch, I see he is wearing her new walking boots. I point at them and look questioningly.

'Boffy is wearing them in for me. You know they were a bit tight. He's a size bigger than me.'

Claire doesn't in any way think this is odd, that this man will crush his feet to be of service to her. She expects it. Boffy looks embarrassed. He would not have wanted anyone else to know.

Jackie's minibus pulls in by the back door. We watch her walk over to Jim. Jackie raises a fist, their knuckles meet and twist. They clap and slap each other's hands. New pictures on the wall, new greetings. What else have I missed?

Jackie does not think Boffy is a strange name. She wants to show him her room and she asks if he has left school. He is coping well. Going with the flow, as they say.

'You don't need to hold his hand, Jackie. He won't try to run away. He won't get far anyway,' Claire says, looking at Boffy flirtatiously as he leaves. Then, to me: 'Well, what do you think?'

What do I think about Boffy, or what do I think she should do? Boffy is lovely but then he would be, trying to impress the family, trying to win her over and get her to move the length of the country to start a new life together. Do I think she should do it? I'm not sure.

'Yes,' I say, nodding towards the door he has left from and doing a thumbs-up sign.

'He is so kind and calm and good for me. He's dreading meeting Mum and Dad, though – and I haven't even warned him about them.'

'Yes,' I say in a calm voice and pat the air downwards to suggest she keeps calm too. George and Shirley are coming round for a meal tonight. Boffy and Claire are going to cook a chicken. She rummages in the fridge to find it and, because it is from the butcher's, there is no label to tell her how heavy it is or how long she needs to cook it for.

'Oh God, I should have asked them.'

'Yes,' I say and gesture for her to hand it to me. I hold the chicken and estimate its weight. 'One, two, three, four.'

'Four kilogram?'

'Yes.' I shake my head and gesture lower.

'Three?'

'Pounds, shillings and pence'.

'Where did that come from?' she says and we both laugh. All these old phrases and lines from songs pop up from some sort of random retrieval system. 'Four pounds?'

'Yes.' Another thumbs-up sign and she's all set. She remembers it's twenty minutes a pound plus twenty minutes.

Boffy and Jackie return and are enlisted for vegetable peeling. I cut up the peeled carrots in the production line. I am still finding more complex tasks difficult – anything that involves working out a sequence. I could quite easily cut up the vegetables and then realise I need to peel them. We work quietly. Claire, in supervisory mode, touches Boffy every time she passes him. They catch one another's eye often. As if conscious of the need to spread herself round, she gives Jackie's shoulders a rub and pats my hand.

Claire talks to Boffy about the political situation, trying to explain Prods and Taigs and UDA and UVF and UFF. He's trying to get his head round the fundamentalist approach of the Paisley Church and asks why they're called *free* Presbyterians.

197

'It sounds anything but free.'

Claire raves about the things she misses like Tayto crisps, Namosa tea and Kimberley biscuits. You can tell she doesn't miss the politics and religion of this place. It's very different to the life she has in London. There, no one is interested in your religion or where your father came from. People live together with no need of marriage.

I am very tired and have an internal debate about whether it is worth the bother of going upstairs for a nap. Everything is still more of an effort than it used to be. I signal what I am going to do by closing my eyes and putting my head to one side, resting on my hand. Life is like a game of charades. In the end it doesn't take that long to get up the stairs, but I get distracted easily and walk into Jackie's room. It's far too small but she never wanted to move and I didn't push it. She has her collections, sticks and stones and pictures from the *Radio Times*. There are a couple of soft toys which she keeps 'in case a wee baby' comes round to play but I know no baby would get their hands on them. She never had the teenage rebellion years so her room remains wholesomely floral and ordered, albeit too cluttered.

I walk into the next room which Claire has commandeered. There are clothes and bags all over the place and lotions and pots with the lids half off. I tidy a little out of habit. She has put Boffy in the room next door, allegedly out of some sort of propriety but I think it's because she couldn't face tidying up.

Claire is going to call me fifteen minutes before Shirley and George arrive. What will they be like in this new situation? Will George be sleazy and suggestive? Will Shirley boss Boffy around and interrogate him? I lie down in the bed and try not to feel too tense to sleep. I lie on my back, not my usual sleeping position, to reinforce the fact that there is no pressure. All I need is a rest. I have rarely rested in this room in daylight since the summer of 1962 when I knew I was pregnant and was terrified my parents would find out. I had heard that pregnant women shouldn't lie on their backs as it would cut the blood supply to your brain so I lay on my back that summer as a suicide attempt. The room has been redecorated several times but somehow the colours and the quality of light have remained the same. The uncertainty and lack of control I felt then is with me again now, but for different reasons.

My memories flip forward and I am here in this bed again. Home from hospital without Jackie, with pressure to leave her there. 'You need never even see her again,' my mother had said. Never see her grow up, never to worry about which is worse, me outliving her or her outliving me. She is twenty-six now but she has already started to look older. They warned me that the ageing process would accelerate for her. Already she has high blood pressure, and every cold seems to turn into a chest infection. She and I might grow old and die at about the same time, despite the twenty-six years between us. But I am too tired to think about that now . .

I wake suddenly when Jackie comes into the room and pushes a piece of paper in my face.

'Claire says you're to come down quick, but not to fall down the stairs,' says Jackie.

The piece of paper is a note in case Jackie forgot what she was supposed to say. They've arrived half an hour early!!!! Can't leave Boff. I need you.

If Jackie helps I'll be able to get up quicker.

'Hand me,' I say, meaning give me a hand or help me.

'What are you talking about?' says Jackie, but she automatically pulls my outstretched arm.

I wanted to be there to help Claire. She had planned to get everything ready before they arrived.

I dress on my own easily now. I try to wear normal things. I want to look nice, not as if I'm convalescing. I have picked out a purple dress I'd usually wear for something special. When I search for a pair of tights, I happen upon a T-shirt tucked in my drawer. It is green and faded; the plasticky logo of some bar in Letterkenny is peeling off. Jim's clothes in my drawer? I don't understand. Looking back over this past few months is like watching a news report where there are crucial details pixelated.

Then suddenly I have this memory of being in Jim's arms in this room and talking about Glasgow and telling him about the baby. I hear Jim, who never got riled about anything, rant about the hard heart of the Ulster Protestants. I feel him hold me so tight I wriggle to loosen his arms so I can breathe. I don't know what this is. Is it a real memory? It feels like déjà vu.

When I get downstairs they are having a discussion. Claire thinks everyone should add their own salt and Shirley thinks a little bit of salt never hurt anybody. Clare is terse but not rude. Her mother's tone is indignant.

George is verbally shuffling around Boffy.

'So what sort of motor do you have?' he asks.

'I don't have a car. I don't really need it where I live,' says Boffy apologetically.

'No car?' George shakes his head as if Boffy has told him he has been recently castrated.

'No one we know has a car. There's no call for it in London,' says Claire looking out for Boffy even while defending her salt policy.

'I'll probably get a car soon,' says Boffy, trying to appease George.

He listens patiently to George's uninterrupted chat about cars and gadgets and tools.

'And we have a great wee cordless electric screwdriver in the shop. It came in today. Powerful easy to use. Even a girl could use it,' George explains.

'Oh, Dad.' Claire turns from the potato mashing. 'How can

you say that? In front of three women, especially Auntie Maureen who has no problems using machinery.'

Even Shirley, hardly a feminist, steps in.'Aye, George, you still haven't mastered the Hoover, have you? A wee bit of practice might help.'

Claire turns to Boffy. 'It's like the Dark Ages here. They're all up in arms if a woman gets a job over a man.'

So for all the romanticising about the place and playing old cassette tapes with songs about the Auld Lammas Fair or The Green Glens of Antrim, I can see she's not going to last long here.

The food arrives and it is plain and good. I wish there was more salt in it, but I am on Claire's side and I'm the one who's had the stroke. I notice that Boffy has been given the cat-food fork but I keep quiet. Jackie is quiet too and then she says, 'Boffy has a dog.'

'Well, it's at my Mum's house.'

'And where do your people live?' asks Shirley.

Boffy's interrogation has begun. Boffy tells us about his life. He lives outside London in Surbiton which we'd heard of because that's where *The Good Life* was set. His mother and father have never lived together. I see George and Shirley glance at each other in the way couples do.

'And why the hell are you called Boffy?' George demands finally, 'You surely weren't christened that.'

'It was a nickname at school and it caught on. Even my mum calls me Boffy.'

'Funny sort of nickname,' sniffs George.

Claire is quick to come to Boffy's rescue. 'He was very clever at school so they started calling him boffin, then Boffy. Okay, Dad?'

23

There was a telephone call at nine o'clock this morning apparently, while I was in the bath. Elizabeth Kelso, asking if ten was a suitable time to visit.

'I hope that's all right,' says Claire. 'You know Mrs Kelso – you feel you haven't got a choice.'

'Yes.'

It's ten now. Claire has tidied up for Elizabeth coming. She and Boffy are snuggled up on the sofa trying to convince Jackie and me to like a band whose music she is playing. I hope they will stay when Elizabeth is here, but I doubt it. Claire feels unforgiven about the break-up of the short-lived engagement to David Kelso all those years ago.

The doorbell rings. This is always a surprise as most people open the door, walk in and give a shout. Claire answers it, ushers Elizabeth in and does an embarrassed 'this is my boyfriend' introduction. Boffy clearly has been briefed about the situation and is stilted in his answers to Elizabeth's polite questions while Claire makes us a pot of coffee and puts it on the table. She tells Elizabeth that they are going to take the dog for a walk. The dog will be surprised because she hardly sits still and has never been 'taken for a walk' in her life.

I hear Claire getting Jackie organised, the shutting of the back door and the dog being called. Elizabeth is silent now and doesn't even make the pretence of pouring the coffee for either of us. She takes a breath as if making a deliberate effort to compose herself. Her lipstick is dark with bluish tones and it reminds me of a girl in my class at school who had a heart condition. She looks straight at me.

'I have come today to ask you to leave my husband alone. I have put up with years of you two making eyes at each other, you sidling over so he has to ask you to dance at parties, you making out that Jacqueline's not well, him stinking of your scent after that party. You needn't think you're special, Maureen. You're just his latest project. He's always got some lame duck to rescue. God, I've turned a blind eye for long enough.'

Elizabeth is shaking. She turns away and her voice drops and becomes more passionate.

'And now, after all the denials, he tells me he's not been happy for years. Now, apparently, he wants to be with you. I have done everything for that man. The house is perfect. I've not let my standards fall, but *you*, Maureen, you walk around like a gypsy most of the time. I half-expect you to be selling pegs. And now you've had a stroke and he's all emotional about it and being ridiculous. If you don't leave him alone, you are even more selfish than I thought.'

Elizabeth has barely paused for breath. Her face is full of fury and distress. I look down at my hands. I just want her to go. Nothing I could say would make any difference anyway. A silent period passes and she gets up and leaves.

Claire bursts in five minutes later.

'Did you hear that? She reversed into the byre wall. She didn't even check the car. Weird, bloody woman. I told you, didn't I, Boffy?'

'I hope she's okay,' says Boffy mildly, neither agreeing or disagreeing.

I shake my head as if in disbelief and exasperation, but I am shaken by the visit. Elizabeth says I'm not the only one. Was she being vindictive?

Claire examines the untouched coffee-pot. 'Our coffee's not good enough for her?'

I close my eyes not to sleep but to opt out of the conversation with Claire but eventually do start to feel sleepy. Any sort of emotional overload seems to shut me down.

I think I have been dozing a while when I hear Boffy speak,

'I really love her, you know, Maureen,' he tells me.

'Yes,' I say in agreement.

'I knew the minute I saw her. It wasn't the same for her, though.'

'Yes?' I say as a question.

"She... I think she thought she could do better. Better than a boffin.'

'Yes?' I try to sound disbelieving.

'But I've grown on her. I don't give up.' Boffy smiles.

'Yes.'

Boffy straightens each finger with his other hand, hyper-extending the joints as if getting ready for some intricate task.

'The job in Edinburgh: I won't take it if she won't come. I haven't told her that. It's a sort of test. I don't want to sound manipulative but I'm hoping it'll help her sort out what she wants. There are temptations in London, other guys hanging around – you know, drama-school types who wear skinny jeans and fedora hats and hold their cigarettes like props. I think she thinks I'll hold her back, but they... Well, they're only in it for themselves. They feed on other people. You wouldn't believe how patronising they are with me.'

This is the longest speech Boffy has made and he looks a bit embarrassed. You can see why therapists sit there and keep quiet. My lack of words has brought this out.

I see it clearly. Claire and he will flourish if she really makes a go of it. If it doesn't work, Boffy won't be the reason. I probably shouldn't have married Walter – but the blame shouldn't lie with him for all my regrets.

'I talked to my mum about things,' says Boffy.

'Yes.' I must have looked or sounded disapproving.

'But I'm not some sort of Mummy's boy,' he adds hastily.

He cares about what I think – and it's not even that he's worried I'll tell Claire. He's a nice lad.

While he chats, I look at him. Boffy is tall and solid. He has an unusual dress sense and no one has told him that horizontal stripes give the illusion of width which he doesn't need. He has a double cow's lick and in the morning his thick hair sticks up; with his stripy jumper he looks like a grown-up Dennis the Menace. I can see why the skinny actors in hats don't bother with him. He has strong-looking hands and is always touching things as if sucking up information about them – everything from the furniture, to the old gate, to Claire. Boffy's eyes are a dark jade colour, and if he looks at you or even sometimes if he thinks he's alone, he's smiling. It's as if his automatic expression is smiling and he'd have to adapt it if he heard bad news.

I've grown to like him. He feels authentic. He let me win at draughts a few times but latterly he has been tougher. Although he has nothing in common with Shirley or George, he has not been tempted into making negative comments about them, despite strong encouragement from Claire. He knows that although you moan about your own family, you don't really want to hear anyone else join in.

Boffy likes carrying things for people. He lifts the groceries in from the car before anyone else gets a chance. He's a boy brought up by a woman alone and he knows his size is an advantage. I picture his mother asking him to lift heavy boxes or put up the Christmas tree the moment he's big enough.

Last night, George left Boffy a copy of *Autocar* to read and marked various pages with strips of kitchen roll. I watched Boffy struggling to unglaze his expression as the conversation progressed.

'You don't even want a car,' Claire said later.

'Well, I might some day and he's trying to help. He knows a lot.'

'He never talks to me about cars,' she said, and I wondered then if she felt jealous. Although she didn't necessarily want it, she could see that a son born into that family would have had a different relationship with her father.

The dog, still unnecessarily pleased to see me back, has taken to sitting outside and watching me through the front-room window as if to prevent me being taken away again. Shirley is worried the dog will knock me over and tries to shoo her away if we're out in the yard. But Tara is steadfast. She keeps her distance, watching me like a benevolent guard, ready to step in if I try to get away, as she did with the litter of pups she had years ago. After our trip in the car the other day we found Tara sitting on the wall at the end of the lane. Claire and Boffy compare her to the legendary Greyfriars Bobby they learned about on their recent trip to Edinburgh. Then they remember that Greyfriars Bobby sat by his master's grave and they backtrack a little.

For a while after the stroke, I didn't care much about food but now I crave things as if I were pregnant. I want things with a bit of bite, horseradish or nose-stinging mustard or peppery salami. I want to feel and taste everything to the full. I want to run, though it's years since I've done that, or swim like I did sometimes with Jim. I want to sing and chat and phone people, but for now I'm only a watcher.

They are all in the kitchen at the moment. With Claire here, there's a lot of laughter and the noise of games like Buckaroo or Kerplunk. We've become a family like Walter and I never managed to be, having routines and in-jokes and tea rotas. Boffy joins in with the dancing competitions and tiddlywinks. Perhaps exciting isn't everything, perhaps easy-going is better. Maybe that's really where Walter was hard work. He was too serious. I like the lightness of Boffy, the jokes, the games. Exciting doesn't last anyway. Claire could do a lot worse.

I am smiling while thinking of Boffy when a car drives into

the yard. I am terrified it's Elizabeth again. The dog leaves the window to check it out. It's George. I hear him blustering and 'How're ye doing?' his way into the kitchen but I can't hear what he is talking about. With George, I always think 'What's he after?'

Claire comes in looking little sheepish.

'Dad says he'll lend us the car so I can show Boffy some of the sights. For an hour or two. He's... Well, he's offered to hang around here while we're away, in case...'

'In case you get up to something?' says George, giving me mock nudges and over-done winks.

I point to all of them and then in the direction of the lane to show that they can all go, that I'm fine. I've not been left alone on the farm before or even alone with Jackie. Although I like the company, part of me misses those quiet moments, just me and Jackie sitting under the rug watching *Heartbeat* on Sunday nights.

It's a fait accompli. They're going out. It's early closing today and Shirley can pick George up later in her car, so there's no rush. I wonder if there will be a difficult moment when Jackie's not invited – but there's no question of that. She hops in the car with the others. So I'm left alone with George.

The moment they leave, he switches the TV on. Not even a pretence at asking if it's okay. There is silence for about ten minutes and then he starts making comments every few minutes.

'Would you look at the arse on that?... Look at yer man there, face as long as a Lurgan spade... If she'd no money she'd never get a young fella like that... You'd not kick him outta bed yourself, would you, Maureen?... Wahey! I could give *her* one. Right over the sofa.'

George goes out to make himself a coffee and comes back with a couple of rounds of toast and a Tupperware box of shortbread and eats his fill. He rubs his belly, untucks his shirt a bit and reaches for the remote control. Here it comes. What does he want?

'Maureen, you and Walter were always careful with money.'

'Yes,' I say automatically rather than in agreement.

'Walter, I know, would have wanted to help out a bit, in times of trouble. Things are tight at the moment. Shirley and I are a wee bit short, what with all the running to the hospital and that. I'm not going to bother her but between you and me, we could sort it out and then obviously – well, we could settle up later. I could get your chequebook if...'

He can see by my face I am not falling for this. Shirley is the one who runs the finance side of things.

I shake my head.

'A couple of hundred even?'

'Shirley – I'll give it to Shirley. Not you,' I say.

George looks as shocked as I feel. A whole sentence. Not planned.

'What?'

'Shirley can ask.'

'Where's this talking coming from? You're not supposed to be able to talk! Do you remember... ? I told you things in confidence, Maureen. I never expected...'

George takes off his glasses and looks out of the window.

'The stuff I told you – all that nonsense is over.'

'You're a weak bastard. You hurt my sister and . . ' I have exhausted my vocabulary like a speaking doll.

'You can't tell Shirley. Not for my sake; for hers.'

I don't respond.

'I'm going out for a walk.'

'Bastard,' I say, after he leaves.

I watch him on his mobile, pacing the front garden, a bit solemn-looking to start with and then smirking and walking in the pointy-toed slow walk of his that I hate. As he prances past the window, he pats Tara, and I catch a few words:

'... lovely girl like you...'

I know he's not talking to the dog.

*

'I want to talk to Shirley.'

Once I'm alone, I say it aloud a couple of times to practise. I don't know what to say first. I want to talk to her, but not when George is around.

It's mid-afternoon when Shirley bustles in. She has brought me some new herbal tonic which she has read about in the paper.

'This'll boost you up. It's apparently not very nice-tasting but it works miracles.'

'I'm not sure your Maureen needs any miracle cures. Am I right, Maureen?' George, having lain low for the last couple of hours, comes in right after Shirley.

Shirley goes off to get a spoon for the bottle of brown tonic she has procured for me. While she's away, he and I look at each other with well-matched loathing. But he knows my secret is nothing to what I have on him. I never encouraged his confidences. He might feel I tricked him, but it was his own doing.

'I have the measure of you,' says George. He looks at me with a face like a soap opera baddie.

'Me too.' I nod to him.

Shirley comes back, locates her glasses and reads the dosage instructions on the back of the bottle. A tablespoon twice a day apparently. She feeds it to me without warning, reminding me of Walter's single-mindedness when getting the cattle drench down a whole batch of calves. I smile, sit up straight and pretend to be Popeye.

'You'll thank me for it,' she laughs. 'I know you don't believe in herbal stuff. But I'm in charge now.' She seems in better spirits than the other day.

I decide not to tell Shirley anything I've learned about George. I worry that the speech will go and I don't want to use it up on something that it might be best not to say. She waves him off with instructions on how to put a casserole in the oven, sits down on the sofa beside me and tuts.

'He's completely handless you know, Maureen. I can't trust him to do a thing about the house.'

'I had another baby.'

'What? No, you didn't have a baby. You're after having a stroke. That's why you were in hospital. But you're all right now.' Shirley looks panicky. She thinks I'm losing my mind.

'I had a baby after school.'

'What do you mean, after school? Maureen, you're fifty.'

'The year after school. In May, I had a baby. I went away.'

'You went to Auntie Helen's.'

'I went to Glasgow.'

'You had a baby? You had a baby then? In... 1963, was it?'

'Yes.'

'The American?'

'Yes.'

'Why did I not know?'

It is interesting the words she uses. 'Why did I not know?' not, 'Why didn't you tell me?' It's as if she is reproaching herself, but she was only seventeen then and going through a Christian Union phase. She spent most of the summer of the Billy romance being bussed to a mission tent at Cushendall. I don't think she thought sex could ever touch our family.

'I should have known. I knew I wasn't hearing the whole story. I was scared you were ill. I thought you were at some sort of... I don't know what I imagined. In Switzerland or somewhere. How long were you away for?'

'One, two, three, four, five, six.'

'You're speaking.' Shirley is grinning. 'I'm so... I didn't even notice.' She does what seems to be an artificial deep breath but I think she is physically affected by what I've said and the fact that I've been able to say it.

'And the baby?'

'A wee girl,' I say, and then I can't stop crying. Shirley puts her arms round me and rocks me like the missionary woman did at the Green Grove. To be honest, it doesn't feel any less painful today than it did all those years ago. Shirley keeps on rocking and pulls a folded tissue from her sleeve. It smells of her and all the feelings are mixed. I am crying for our lost years together as well as about the first baby.

'We could try to find her,' says Shirley in a soothing voice. 'She'd be in the mid-thirties now. You might even have grandchildren.'

I shake my head wearily. Not now, I think. Not tempting, is it? 'Would you like to meet the mother that deserted you? And your Down's Syndrome sister? By the way, your mum's a stroke victim and can hardly string a sentence together.' It would all look a bit like a dying wish now rather than positively wanting to meet her.

'When did you start talking? No one called me.'

'I just started. I'm – I saved it.' I don't know what I mean but she looks happy.

'That's grand. We can talk. We can talk now. I thought I'd lost you for good.' She pats her chest and breathes deeply. 'I'm sorry about the baby. A big secret. You could have told me. Sure, it could happen to anybody. Well anybody who – you know. George and I – we took risks. Well, you can imagine what George was like then, randy old devil. We didn't wait until the wedding night. I'm no saint either.'

'Yes,' I nod and we both smile.

'Why didn't you tell me?'

'Mother.'

'She was hard, wasn't she? Hard in a lot of ways, thinking back.'

'Yes.'

'She must have been raging with you?'

'Yes. Absolutely.'

Shirley is silent for a while. She fiddles with the clasp of her watch-strap. She folds up the sleeves of her cardigan and then unfolds them. The dog arrives at the window and looks in at me. Shirley walks over and speaks to her.

'Don't worry, Tara, she's still here.' Shirley stands silhouetted at the window. 'I rambled on a bit when I didn't get answers from you. I probably said things I wouldn't have.'

'It's secure.' I'm not sure where the words come from at times.

'We'll be sisters again.'

I know what she means. It's not just sisters again since the stroke happened. It's sisters for the first time since way back. We sit in silence as the room gets darker. Shirley turns the side lights on.

'How long did you have the baby with you?'

'One hour.'

'That's terrible, or I don't know... maybe it's easier?'

'Terrible. Too terrible.'

'Did Walter know?'

I shake my head.

'Who knows?' Shirley is worried that other people have known before her. She's still competitive.

'Tom Kelso. Only him.'

'Oh'. She is quiet but I know there's stuff she wants to ask about him too.

There is the sound of the car in the yard and Claire's gearbox-wrecking parking technique. She, Boffy and Jackie clatter through the kitchen and into the front room with shells and driftwood and a box of buns from the bakery.

'Maureen's speech is coming back. She's a bit slow still but it's coming. Slowly, slowly. Isn't that great? Will we have a drink? Are you allowed to drink? I don't want to set you back. There's some fizzy wine in the larder. Boffy, run and get it, darlin'.' Shirley is ecstatic. There is a lot of hugging and toasting and Jackie is happy too, but you can see she's not sure what the fuss is about.

Shirley is reluctant to leave in case I stop talking. She has alternated between wanting me to save my speech and telling me to keep chatting in case I lose it again. It is a relief when she goes as I think she might have kept me up all night in case I fall asleep and wake speechless again.

'So what do you really think about Boffy?' asks Claire, eager to hear me speak, to hear my opinion.

'Fantastic. A fantastic man.'

'Are you just saying that?'

I shake my head. I still can't say, 'No,' for some reason.

'Will it work? Will we stay together, do you think? Should I move up to Edinburgh with him? Has he said anything to you?'

I ignore the last question.

'Where's my crystal... crystal...' I mime the shape of a crystal ball, even though I know what I want to say.

'I know.' She picks at her fingers and trims a nail with her strong white teeth.

'A good chance,' I say, but the responsibility sits heavy. What do I know really? 'Do you love Boffy?'

'Yes, but how can you tell if you always will?'

'Decide. Make the decision. And hard work.'

Claire decides we need tea after all that booze and goes into the kitchen. Boffy comes in and the two of us sit listening to the news. Now Boffy can ask me questions.

'What's Drumcree? What is a "tay shock"? Why were there no Catholics in the police? Why do you not have Guy Fawkes' Night here? Is Derryconnor a Protestant town?'

I find talking tiring and I use unfamiliar and archaic words and then leave some out.

'Derryconnor is... Stencil,' and then I go on to indicate it's a different word.

'Staunch?' asks Boffy, 'Staunch Protestant?'

'Yes.'

'Okay.' Then: 'Has Claire talked to you about things?'

I put my finger to my lips.

'You're keeping quiet?'

'Yes. Quiet for everybody.'

24

I can hear them speaking very softly.

'Yes, she's still breathing,' says Boffy. 'Leave her to sleep and stop worrying. We went to bed late last night, that's all.'

I can hear the love in his voice. I think about what I told Claire last night about relationships. 'Make the decision and work hard.' But I didn't tell her that both of you had to do that. Walter had made the decision; I'm not sure I really had. He and I were not working together. We had no shared understanding of marriage. And so I began looking elsewhere for solutions. What if Boffy has to fight a Tom Kelso? I think how hurt he would be if Claire was always thinking of leaving him for someone else, and I think what I've done over the years. I would harshly judge the women who try to take George away from Shirley or any woman who was hoping to take Boffy away from Claire.

Why have I been so easy on myself?

I feel low and am slow to get up and down the stairs. The euphoria and excitement of speaking to them all felt like a fresh start last night but this morning, the alcohol and impact of Elizabeth's outburst have dulled my spirits. The warm kitchen and the young people's chat cheers me a bit. Boffy loves Claire's accent and tries to mimic it. He makes her repeat words for his delight. I think in London she probably sounds very different. He does a passable impersonation of Walter Love on Radio Ulster but his Paisley impersonation sounds half-man half-gravel.

'I'm glad you haven't heard me speak enough to start imitating me.'

'I'm slightly disappointed,' says Boffy, teasing. 'Claire told me you were the posh one of the family.'

Claire flits about tidying. On the sideboard she has placed a pile of random items. Among them is a book I borrowed from the hospital and a biscuit tin (now empty) waiting to be retrieved by Sandra Pollock from the church. This area has become the designated lost property department. The remnants of Jackie's raggedy security blanket also lies there, reminding me again of that night with Tom Kelso. Claire tells me Jim wants to come in and see me again.

'I told him you don't need to be bothered by farm stuff but he says he wants to run some things past you.'

Because Jim wants to talk to me I start to worry about the farm as Claire feared I might.

'What does Jim want? Is it all okay?' I point to the world outdoors.

'It seems to be. Jim doesn't say much, does he? He gets on with things. Mum gives him orders every now and then and he does what he's told.'

'Your mother doesn't give him a chance to speak.'

'They have very different styles! I'll tell him to come in any time then?'

Boffy is sitting in the front room reading the paper when Jim comes in and Claire is still tidying up. She is more like her mother than she would like to think. She goes to put the kettle on for Jim and me.

'You have a rest, Claire. Sit down and put your feet up. I'll make Jim a cup of tea.'

'I heard about your speech,' says Jim. 'Very good. You can tell me what you want done about the field by the lake and should I...' He lifts something from the sideboard. It's the scarf from the hospital. Claire has left it there for Tom Kelso to claim. 'I wondered where this had gone.'

'Are you sure it's yours? It was at the hospital. We thought Dr Kelso left it.'

'It's mine. I recognise my sewing.'

He shows me a clumsy darn in brown thread on the edge of the green scarf and now I think about it, I realise Elizabeth Kelso wouldn't let Tom out in it.

'But it was at the hospital.'

'I was there. You don't remember? They rang here – the hospital. The house phone rang so many times that day, I finally came in and answered it. By the time I got through to Shirley, she'd heard. She had to wait for Jackie so I... I hopped on the bike and went down. I never said, because – well, Shirley might have thought I was overstepping. I thought you needed someone and she wasn't able to get down.'

'I don't remember at all.'

'You were all hooked up to drips and heart machines.'

'You were there. It's strange... We wondered about the scarf. I'm glad you came. Sorry I didn't even know.'

'Oh, you're all right there, Maureen.'

'Thanks anyway.'

I finish making the tea. Jim takes off his old parka and tries to look at home.

'It's nice being here with you.'

'Well, I usually went to yours for afternoon tea.' Even now I can't resist flirting.

'We had some good times.'

'We did have good times.'

We look at one another and smile.

'I'm still here,' he says.

I fuss with the tea like a little girl trusted for the first time to use the kettle.

Jim moseys over to the stove and stands beside me while the tea draws. He seems less shy than he used to be.

'How're you really doing, Maureen?'

'I'm doing okay, Jim.'

'I'm staying… if I'm wanted. Shirley has me on the car insurance.'

'*Driving Miss Maureen.*' I'm amazed by my own wit.

He laughs too. He talks about the farm and various bits of gossip and he tells me about Shirley making him wash the yard with a power hose before I got home. It sounds like how they are at school before an inspection. He stops for a moment and I think he is about to go, but then I get the feeling this is what he has really come to talk about.

'Do you remember everything? Before… before you went into hospital?'

'It's mysterious.'

'Mysterious?' He gives me one of his flirty looks, 'How much time is a mystery?'

'Who knows? I think I remember the twelfth of July.'

'But which year?' he jokes.

'It was definitely this past summer.'

'Oh okay. You don't remember…'

'What?'

There is a noise of boots being scraped in the yard.

'Oh, nothing. Nothing to worry about. Everything's grand. Look – I'm heading on.'

He touches my hand in a connecting way that men like him don't usually do. Claire is coming in as he leaves. I don't feel worried about this conversation. He seemed calm and smiling and mild. Watching him leave, I know that there is more to remember.

'That Jim was never off the phone when you were in the hospital, you know,' says Claire, 'Boffy was helping him move something yesterday. He says he seems very fond of you. Has he no family of his own?'

I feel a bit indignant. Claire thinks Jim sees me as a mother figure. Lovely flirty Jim. He never flirts with Claire though.

25

Tom's car is in the yard and I am standing doing the dishes. I'll always have a weakness in this arm but I can do most things. He locks the car door even out here. He always does it in case someone gets hold of his prescription pad.

This is like old times. Claire helped me put a PVC apron on before she left and I can't get it off in time. When she leaves for good, I'll never get it off. I am still fiddling with it when Tom comes in

'Turn round. I'll undo it,' he says.

Never has untying apron-strings felt so intimate. I feel his head against the middle of my back for an instant but something doesn't feel right. Is it what Elizabeth said – or is it to do with Jim?

'Is Claire out?'

I nod.

He does a squeeze of my left hand. I try to squeeze back.

'Better. It gets better every time I see you.' He takes the other hand too but stops pretending he's interested in my health. 'Maureen, come away with me. We've got nothing to lose. I don't give a damn about what they'll all say.'

I am still and hot with emotion. I think of Elizabeth and what this would do to her. The shame for Shirley. Nothing to lose? He has everything to lose – his job, his marriage, quite probably his sons' respect. And although I'm all right now, what is in store for me?

'Maureen, will you come away with me?'

'Yes,' I say, but he can tell it's not a real yes.

He asks again.

'Will you come away with me?'
'No.'

The End

Acknowledgements

Thank you to Silvertail Books for publishing this, my first novel.

Sincere thanks to all those who have helped me in my writing along the way. Mary Doherty and Ann Vaughan Williams were two of many inspiring teachers. Virginia West helped me to see that I needed to leave the housework and finish the book.

I am grateful for all the support, ideas and tea provided by my friends and family. Many of them have read early versions of *Yes* and given insightful advice. Thanks to Tania, for guidance about writing the scenes about occupational therapy. Thank you to my book group for generously treating my first finished draft like a real book. Thank you to Molly, Sam and Ratan for not letting me give up.

A special thanks to my band of fellow writers. It has been ten years since we first met on an Arvon Course. They have been a source of great encouragement and laughter.